The Tail of Emily Windsnap

Also by Liz Kessler

Emily Windsnap and the Monster from the Deep

The Tail of Emily Windsnap

LIZ KESSLER

Decorations by Sarah Gibb

Dolphin Paperbacks

First published in Great Britain in 2003
by Orion Children's Books
This edition published 2004 by Dolphin paperbacks
a division of the Orion Publishing Group Ltd
Orion House
5 Upper St Martin's Lane
London WC2H 9EA

10 9 8 7

Text © Liz Kessler 2003
Illustrations © Sarah Gibb 2003

The right of Liz Kessler and Sarah Gibb to be
identified as the author and illustrator respectively
of this work has been asserted.

The Orion Publishing Group's policy is to use papers that
are natural, renewable and recyclable products and
made from wood grown in sustainable forests. The logging
and manufacturing processes are expected to conform to
the environmental regulations of the country of origin.

A catalogue record for this book is
available from the British Library.

Printed in Great Britain by
Clays Ltd, St Ives plc

ISBN-10 1 84255 166 3
ISBN-13 978 1 84255 166 0

For Frankie, Lucy and Emily
And for Dad

Come, dear children, let us away;
Down and away below.
Now my brothers call from the bay;
Now the great winds shoreward blow;
Now the salt tides seaward flow;
Now the wild white horses play,
Champ and chafe and toss in the spray.
Children dear, let us away.
This way, this way!

from The Forsaken Merman,
by Matthew Arnold

Chapter One

*C*an you keep a secret?

I know everyone has secrets but mine's different. Kind of weird. Sometimes I have nightmares where I get found out and locked up in a zoo or a scientist's laboratory.

It all started in Year Seven when swimming lessons began. It was the first Wednesday afternoon at my new school and I was so looking forward to it. Mum hates swimming and always used to change the subject when I asked why I couldn't learn.

'But we live on a boat!' I'd say. 'We're surrounded by water!'

'You're not getting me in there,' she'd reply. 'Just look at all the pollution. You know what it's like when the day cruises have been in. Now stop arguing and come and help me with the vegetables.'

She even kept me out of swimming lessons all the way through primary school. Said it was unhealthy. 'All those bodies mixing in the same water,' she'd shudder, 'not for *us* thank you very much.'

And that would be that: end of discussion. I finally wore her down the summer before I started secondary school. 'All right, all right,' she sighed, eventually. 'I give in. Just don't start trying to get *me* in there with you.'

I'd never been in the sea. I'd never even had a bath. I'm not dirty or anything – I have a shower every night. But there isn't enough room for a bath on the boat, so I'd never been totally *immersed* in water.

Till the first Wednesday afternoon of Year Seven.

Mum bought me a new bag especially for my costume and towel. On the side, it had a picture of a woman doing front crawl. I looked at the picture and dreamed about winning Olympic races, with a Speedo costume and black goggles just like hers.

Only it didn't quite happen like that.

When we got to the baths, a man with a whistle and white shorts and a red T-shirt told the girls to go in one room and the boys to go in the other.

I changed quickly in the corner. I didn't want anyone to see my skinny body. My legs are like sticks and they're usually covered in scabs and grazes from getting on and off *The King of the Sea*. That's our boat. Which is a bit of a grand title for a little sailing boat with mouldy ropes, peeling paint and beds the width of a ruler. But anyway. We usually just call it *King*.

Julie Crossens smiled at me as she put her clothes in her locker. 'I like your cozzy,' she said. It's just plain black with a white stripe across the middle.

'I like your hat,' I smiled back as she squashed her hair into her tight, pink swimming cap. I squeezed my ponytail under mine. I usually wear my hair loose; Mum made me put it in a bobble today. It's mousy brown and used to be short but I'm growing it at the moment. It's a bit longer than shoulder length so far.

Julie and I sit next to each other sometimes. We're not best friends. Sharon Matterson used to be my best friend but she went to Our Lady. I'm at Bright-port High. Julie's the only person I might want to be best friends with. I think she wants to be Mandy Rushton's, though. They hang out together at break.

I don't mind. Not really. Except when I can't find my way to the canteen – or to some of the classes. It might be nice to have someone to get lost with.

Brightport High is about ten times bigger than my primary school! It's like an enormous maze, with MILLIONS of boys and girls who all seem to know what they're doing.

'You coming, Julie?' Mandy Rushton stood between us with her back to me. She gave me a quick look, then she whispered something in Julie's ear and laughed. Julie didn't look up as they passed me.

Mandy lives on the pier, like me. Her parents run the amusement arcade and they've got a flat above it. We used to be quite friendly till last year when I accidentally told my mum that Mandy had showed me how to win free goes on the one-armed bandit. I didn't *mean* to get her in trouble but – well, let's just say I'm not exactly welcome in the amusements any more. In fact, she hasn't spoken to me ever since.

And now we've ended up in the same class at Brightport High. Brilliant. As if starting a new school the size of a city isn't bad enough.

I finished getting ready on my own.

'OK, listen up, 7C,' the man with the whistle said. He told us to call him Bob. 'Any of you kids totally confident to swim on your own?'

'Course we can – we're not babies!' Mandy sneered under her breath.

Bob turned to face her. 'All right then. Do you

want to start us off? Let's see what you can do.'

Mandy stepped towards the pool. She stuck her thumb in her mouth. 'Ooh, look at me. I'm a baby. I can't swim!' Then she dropped herself sideways into the water. Her thumb still in her mouth, she pretended to slip under as she did this really over the top kind of doggy paddle across the pool.

Half the class were laughing by the time she reached the end.

Bob wasn't. His face reddened. 'Do you think that's funny? Get out! Now!' he shouted. Mandy pulled herself out and grinned as she bowed to the class.

'You *silly* girl,' Bob handed her a towel. 'You can sit on the side and watch.'

'*What?*' Mandy stopped grinning. 'That's not fair! What did I do?'

Bob turned his back on her. 'Now, we'll start again. Who's happy to swim confidently *and* sensibly?'

About three-quarters of the class raised their hands. I was desperate to get in the pool but didn't dare put mine up. Not after that.

'Right then.' Bob nodded at them. 'You can get in if you want – but just in the shallow end, mind.'

He turned back to the rest of the class who were lined up and shivering by the side of the pool. 'I'll start with this lot.'

Once his back was turned, I couldn't stop myself. I sneaked in with the group making their way round to the shallow end! I'd never swum before so I shouldn't have, but I just knew I could do it. And the water looked *so* beautiful lying there, still and calm, as though it was holding its breath waiting for someone to jump in and set it alive with splashes and ripples.

There were five big steps that led gradually into the water. I stepped onto the first one and warm water tickled over my toes. Another step and the water wobbled over my knees. Two more, then I pushed myself into the water.

I ducked my head under, reaching wide with my arms. As I held my breath and swam deeper, the silence of the water surrounded me and called to me, drawing my body through its creamy calm. It was as if I'd found a new home.

'Now THAT is more like it!' Bob shouted when I came up for air. 'You're a natural!'

Then he turned back to the others, squinting and staring at me with open mouths. Mandy's eyes fired hatred at me as Bob said, 'That's what I'd like to see you *all* doing by the end of the term.'

And then it happened.

One minute, I was skimming along like a flying fish. The next, my legs suddenly seized up. It felt as though someone had glued my thighs together and strapped a splint on my shins! I tried to smile as I paddled to the side but my legs had turned to a block of stone! I couldn't feel my knees, my feet, my toes. *What was happening?*

A second later, I almost went under completely and I screamed. Bob dived in, in his shorts and T-shirt, and swam over to me.

'It's my legs,' I gasped. 'I can't feel them!'

He cupped my chin in his big hand and back-stroked us to the side. 'Don't worry,' he said, looking behind us as he swam. 'It's just cramp. Happens to everyone.'

We reached the big steps at the side of the pool and sat down on the top one. As soon as I was halfway out of the water, the weird feeling started to go away.

'Now, let's have a look at those legs.' Bob lifted me onto the side of the pool. 'Can you lift your left one up?' I did.

'And your right?' Easy.

'Any pain?'

'It's gone,' I said.

'Just a bit of cramp, then. Why don't you have a rest here for a few minutes? Get in again when you're ready?'

I nodded and he went back to the others.

But I'd felt something that he hadn't seen. And I'd seen something that he hadn't felt. And I didn't have a *clue* what it was but I knew one thing for sure – you wouldn't get me back in that pool for a million pounds.

I sat by the side for a long time. All the rest of the class eventually got in and started splashing about. Even Mandy was allowed back in. But I didn't want to sit too near in case I got splashed and it happened again. I was even nervous when I went home after school in case I fell off the jetty into the sea.

The jetties are all along one side of the pier. There are three other boats on ours. A posh white speed-boat and a couple of bigger yachts. None of the others have people living on them though.

I stepped onto the jetty. We've got this old plank of wood that we put across to the boat. Mum used to carry me over it when I was little but I'd been doing it on my own for ages. Only, I couldn't that day. I called her from the jetty.

'I can't get across,' I shouted when she came up from below deck.

She had a towel wrapped round her head and a satin dressing-gown on. 'I'm getting ready for my book group.'

I stood frozen on the jetty. Around me, the boats melted into a wobbly mass of poles and sails. I stared at *King*. The sail was down. The mast rocked with the boat, the wooden deck shiny with sea spray. My eyes blurred as I focused on the row of portholes along the side of the boat; the thin metal bar running round the edge. 'I'm scared,' I said.

Eventually, Mum pulled the dressing-gown cord tighter round her waist and reached her skinny arm out to me. 'Come on then, let's have you.'

When I got across, she grabbed me and gave me a hug. 'Dingbat,' she said, ruffling my hair. Then she went back inside to get ready for her group.

Mum's always got some group or other on the go. Last year it was pilates; now it's her book group. She works at the secondhand bookshop on the promenade. That's where they meet. It's pretty cool, actually. They've just opened up a café bar where you can get thick milkshakes with real fruit in them and huge wodges of chocolate flapjack. I reckon the book group is just her latest excuse to meet up and gossip with her friends – but at least it keeps her off my back.

Mystic Millie who does Palms on the Pier comes and sits with me. Millie's all right. Sometimes she practises reiki or shiatsu on me. She brought her tarot cards round once. Said I was about to achieve academic success and win praise from all quarters. The next day I came bottom in the spelling test and was given three lunchtime detentions to catch up. But that's Millie for you.

Luckily, *Emmerdale* and *EastEnders* were both on tonight so I knew she wouldn't bother me. Just as well because I wanted to be left alone. I needed time to think about what to do. There were two things I knew for sure. One: I had to work out what had happened to me in the pool. And two: I needed to get out of swimming lessons before it happened again.

9

I could hear Mum in her cabin while I paced up and down in the front room. *'Do ya really love me? Do ya wanna stay?'* she was singing louder than her CD. She always sings when she's getting ready to go out. I don't mind too much – except when she starts on the actions. Tonight, I hardly noticed.

I'd already tried asking her if I had to go swimming again and she went mad. 'I hope you're joking,' she'd said in that voice that means *she* isn't. 'After the fuss you created – *no way* are you giving up now!'

I paced up to the gas fire in the corner of the saloon. That's what we call the living room. I usually get my best ideas when I pace but nothing was coming to me. I paced past the tatty old sofa with a big orange blanket. Pace, pace, left, right, creak, squeak, think, think. Nothing.

'Better tell me soon, baby I ain't got all day.' Mum's voice warbled out from her room.

I tried extending my pacing to the kitchen. It's called a galley, really. It's got a sink, a tiny fridge and a cooking surface that's always covered in empty cartons and bottles. Mum makes us recycle *everything*. The galley's in the middle of the boat with the main door and a couple of wooden steps opposite. You've got to be careful on these when you come in, because the bottom step comes loose. I usually jump down from the top one.

I paced through the kitchen and along the corridor that leads to the bathroom and our cabins.

'How do I look?' Mum appeared at the end of the corridor. She was wearing a new pair of Levis and a white T-shirt with 'BABE' in sparkly letters across the middle. I wouldn't mind but I bought a similar one myself at the same time – and it looks better on her!

'Great.' A familiar sharp rap on the roof stopped me saying any more. The side door opened and Mr Beeston poked his head through. 'Only me,' he called, peering round the boat.

Mr Beeston's the lighthouse keeper. He comes round all the time. He gives me the creeps – he kind of looks at you out of the corner of his eyes when he's talking to you. And they're different colours: one's blue, one's green. Mum says he probably gets lonely in his lighthouse, sitting around looking out to sea, switching the light on, only having contact with people by radio. That's why he's always popping in. She says we have to be friendly to him.

'Oh, Mr Beeston, I'm just off out to my book group. We're waiting for Millie to turn up. Come in a sec. I'll walk down with you.' Mum disappeared down the corridor to get her coat as he clambered through the door.

'And how are we?' he asked, staring sideways into my eyes. His mouth was crooked like his tie. His shirt was missing a button, his mouth missing a tooth. I shivered. I wish Mum wouldn't leave me on my own with him.

'Fine, thanks.'

He narrowed his eyes, still staring at me. 'Good, good.'

Thankfully, Millie arrived a minute later and Mum and Mr Beeston went out.

'I won't be late, darling,' Mum said, kissing my cheek then wiping it with her thumb. 'There's shepherd's pie in the oven. Help yourselves.'

'Hi Emily.' Millie looked at me intensely for a moment. She always does that. 'You're feeling anxious and confused,' she said with alarming accuracy for once. 'I can see it in your aura.'

Then she swept her black cape over her shoulder and put the kettle on.

I waved goodbye as Mum and Mr Beeston headed down the pier. At the bottom, Mr Beeston turned left to walk round the bay, back to his lighthouse. The streetlamps lining the prom were already on, pale yellow spots against an orangey-pink sky. Mum turned right for the bookshop.

I watched till they'd gone out of sight before joining Millie on the sofa. We had the shepherd's pie on our knees and laughed together at the weatherman when he fluffed his lines. Then *Emmerdale* started and she shushed me and went all serious.

I had an hour.

I cleared the plates, then raided the pen jam jar, got

a sheet of Mum's posh purple writing paper from the living room cupboard and shut myself in my cabin.

This is what I wrote:

> *Dear Mrs Partington*
> *Please can you let Emily off her swimming lessons. We have been to the doctor and he says she has a bad allergy and MUST NOT go near water. At all. EVER.*
> *Kindest wishes*
> *Mary Penelope Windsnap*

I pretended to be asleep when I heard Mum come in. She tiptoed into my room, kissed me on top of my head and smoothed the hair off my forehead. She always does that. I wish she wouldn't. I hate having my fringe pushed off my forehead but I stopped myself from pulling it back till she'd gone.

I lay awake for hours. I've got some fluorescent stars and a crescent moon on my ceiling and I looked up at them, trying to make sense of what had happened.

All I really wanted to think about was the silkiness of the water as I sliced through it – before everything went wrong. I could still hear its silence pulling me, playing with me as though we shared a secret. But every time I started to lose myself to the feeling of its creamy warmth on my skin, Mandy's face broke into the picture. Glaring at me. A couple of times I almost fell asleep. Drifting into panicky half-dreams – me inside a huge tank, all the class around me, pointing, staring, chanting: 'Freak! Freak!'

I could *never* go in the water again!

But the questions wouldn't leave me alone. What had *happened* to me in there? Would it happen again?

And no matter how much I dreaded the idea of putting myself through that terror again, I knew I would never be happy until I had the answers. More than that, something was simply pulling me back to the water. It was like I didn't have a choice. I HAD to find out – however scary it might be.

By the time I heard Mum's gentle snores coming from her room, I was determined to get to the bottom of it – before anyone else did.

I crept out of bed and slipped into my swimming costume. It was still damp and I winced and pulled my denim jacket over the top. Then I tiptoed out of the boat and looked round. The pier was totally deserted. Along the prom, guesthouses and shops stood in a silent row of silhouettes against the night sky. They could have been a stage set.

A great big full moon shone a spotlight across the sea. I felt sick as I looked at the plank of wood, stretching across to the jetty. *Come on, just a couple of steps.*

I clenched my teeth and my fists – and tiptoed across.

I ran to the bollards at the end of the pier and looked down at the rope ladder stretching into the darkness of the water. The sea glinted coldly at me; I shivered in reply. Why was I doing this?

I wound my fingers round my hair. I always do that when I'm trying to think – if I don't feel like pacing. And then I pushed the questions and the doubts – and Mandy's sneering face – out of my mind. I *had* to do it, had to know the truth.

I buttoned up my jacket. I wasn't getting in there without it on! Holding my breath, I stepped onto the rope ladder and looked out at the deserted pier one last time. I could hear the gentle chatter of masts clinking in the bay as I carefully made my way down into the darkness.

The last step of the rope ladder was still quite a way from the sea because the tide was out. *It's now or never*, I said to myself.

Then, before I had time to think another thought, I pinched my nose between my thumb and forefinger – and jumped.

I landed in the water with a heavy splash and gasped for breath as soon as I came up. At first I couldn't feel anything, except the freezing cold water. *What on earth was I doing?*

Then I remembered what I was there for and started kicking my legs. A bit frantically at first. But seconds later, the cold melted away and so did my worries. Instead, a feeling of calm washed over me with the waves. Salt on my lips, hair flat against my head, I darted under the surface, cutting through the water as though I lived there.

And then – IT – happened. I swam straight back to the pier, terrified. NO! I didn't want this – I'd changed my mind!

I reached out but couldn't get hold of the ladder. *What had I done?* My legs were joining together again, turning to stone! I gasped and threw my arms about uselessly, clutching at nothing. *Just cramp, just cramp*, I told myself, not daring to look as my legs disappeared altogether.

But then, as rapidly as it had started, something changed; I stopped fighting it.

OK, so my legs had joined together. And fine, now they had disappeared completely. So what? It was good. It was . . . right.

As soon as I stopped worrying, my head stopped slipping below the surface. My arms stopped flailing about everywhere. Suddenly I was an eagle, an aeroplane – a dolphin, gliding through the water for the sheer pleasure of it.

Right, this is it. You might have guessed by now or you might not. It doesn't matter. All that matters is that you promise never to tell anyone.

I had become a mermaid.

Chapter Two

*I*t's not exactly the kind of thing that happens every day, is it? It doesn't happen *at all* to most people. But it happened to me. I was a mermaid. A mermaid! How did it happen? Why? Would I always be one? Questions filled my head, but I couldn't answer a single one. All I knew was that I'd discovered a whole new part of myself and nothing I'd ever done in my life had felt so good.

So there I was, swimming like – well, like a fish! And in a way, I *was* a fish. My top half was the same as usual; skinny little arms, my fringe plastered to my forehead with seawater, black Speedo cozzy.

But then, just below the white line that goes across my tummy, I was someone else; something else. My costume melted away and, instead, I had shiny scales. My legs narrowed into a long, gleaming, purple and green tail, waving gracefully as I skimmed along in the water. I'd never done anything gracefully in my life so it was a bit of a shock! When I flicked my tail above the surface, it flashed an arc of rainbow colours in the moonlight. I could zoom through the water with the tiniest movement, going deeper and deeper with every flick of my tail.

It reminded me of the time we went to World of Water with school. We were in a tunnel under the water with sea life all around us. It felt as if we were really in the sea. Only, this time I was! I could reach out and touch the weeds floating up through the water, upside-down beaded curtains. I could race along with the fat grey fish grouped together in gangs, weaving around each other as though they were dancing.

I laughed with pleasure and a line of bubbles escaped from my mouth, climbing up to the surface.

It seemed as though I'd only been swimming for five minutes when I realised the sky was starting to grow pink. I panicked as a new thought hit me: *what if I couldn't turn back?*

But the second I'd pulled myself out of the water, my tail softened. I dangled on the rope ladder and watched, fascinated, as the shiny scales melted away, one by one. As my legs returned, they felt odd, like when your mouth goes numb after you've had a filling.

I wiggled my toes to get rid of the pins and needles in my feet. Then I headed home with a promise to myself that I would be back – soon.

Bob, the swimming instructor, was standing in front of me, talking into a mobile phone. I couldn't hear what he was saying. Someone grabbed my shoulders.

'This the one, is it?' a snarling voice growled behind my ear. Bob nodded.

I tried to wriggle free from the man's clutches but he was holding my shoulders too firmly. 'What do you want?' a voice squeaked from my mouth.

'As if you didn't know,' the snarly voice snapped at me. 'You're the freak.' He shook my shoulders.

'I'm not a freak,' I shouted. 'I'm not!'

'Stop pretending,' a woman's voice replied.

'I'm not pretending,' I wriggled under the hands holding my shoulders. 'I'm not a freak!'

'Emily, for pete's sake,' the woman's voice said. 'I know you're not really asleep.'

My eyes snapped open to see Mum's face inches from mine, her hands on my shoulders, shaking me gently. I bolted upright in my bed. 'What's happening?'

Mum let go of me. 'What's happening, dozy drawers, is that you're going to be late for school. Now get a move on.' She parted the curtain in the doorway. 'And don't forget to brush your teeth,' she said without turning round.

Over breakfast, I tried to remember my dream and

the things I'd been shouting. It had felt so real: the capture, the voices. Had I said anything out loud? I didn't dare ask so I ate in silence.

It was on the third mouthful that things went seriously wrong.

Mum was fussing around as usual, shuffling through the huge pile of papers stuffed behind the mixer. 'What did I do with it?'

'What is it this time?'

'My shopping list. I'm sure I put it down here somewhere.' She leaned across to a pile of papers on the table. 'Ah, here it is.'

I looked up in horror as she picked up a piece of paper. Not just any piece of paper. A SHEET OF POSH PURPLE WRITING PAPER!

'No-o-o-o!' I yelped, spitting half a mouthful of cereal across the table and leaping forward to grab the paper. Too late. She was unfolding it.

Her eyes narrowed as she scanned the sheet and I held my breath.

'No, that's not it.' Mum started to fold the paper up. I breathed out and swallowed the rest of my mouthful.

But then she opened it again. 'Hang on a sec. That's my name there.'

'No, no, it's not. It's someone else, it's not you at all!' I snatched at the paper.

Mum ignored me. 'Where are my reading glasses?' They were round her neck – as they usually are when she's looking for them.

'Why don't I read it to you?' I said, in my best Perfect Daughter voice. But as I was speaking, she found her glasses and put them on. She studied the note.

I tried to edge away from the table but she looked up on my second step. '*Emily*?'

'Hm?'

She took her glasses off and waved the note in front of my face. 'Want to explain this to me?'

'Ah, well, hm, ah, er, let's see now.' I examined the note with what I hoped was an I've-never-seen-it-in-my-life-before-but-I'll-see-if-I-can-help kind of expression on my face.

She didn't say anything and I kept staring at the note, pretending I was reading it. Anything to avoid meeting her eyes while I waited for my telling off.

But then she did something even worse than tell me off. She put the piece of paper down, lifted my chin up with her hand and said, 'I understand, Emily. I know what it's about.'

'You do?' I squeaked, terrified.

'All those things you were saying in your sleep about being a freak. I should have realised.'

'You should?'

She let go of my chin and shook her head sadly. 'I've been an idiot not to realise before now.'

'You have?'

Then she took my hand between her palms and said, 'You're like me. You're afraid of water.'

'I am?' I squealed. Then I cleared my throat and

straightened my school tie. 'I mean, I *am*,' I said seriously. 'Of course I am! I'm scared of water. That's exactly what I am. That's what this has all been about. Just that, nothing more than –'

'Why didn't you tell me?'

I looked down at my lap and closed my eyes tight, trying to squeeze a bit of moisture out of them. 'I was ashamed,' I said quietly. 'I didn't want to let you down.'

Mum pressed my hand harder between hers and looked into my eyes. Hers were a bit wet, too. 'It's all my fault,' she said. 'I'm the one who's let *you* down. I stopped you from learning to swim and now you've inherited my fear.'

'Yes,' I nodded sadly. 'I suppose I have. But you mustn't blame yourself. It's OK. I don't mind, honestly.'

She let go of my hand and shook her head. 'But we live on a boat,' she said. 'We're surrounded by water.'

I almost laughed, but stopped myself when I saw the serious expression on her face. Then a thought occurred to me. 'Mum, why exactly *do* we live on a boat if you're so afraid of water?'

She screwed up her eyes, stared into mine as if she was looking for something. 'I know,' she whispered. 'I can't explain it, but it's such a deep feeling – I could *never* leave *King*.'

'But it doesn't make any sense. I mean, you're scared of water and we live on a boat in a seaside town!'

'I know, I know!'

'We're miles from anywhere. Even Nan and Grandad live at the other end of the country.'

Mum's face hardened. 'Nan and Grandad? What have they got to do with it?'

'I've never even seen them! Two cards a year and that's it.'

'I've told you before, Em. They're a long way away. And we're not – we don't get on too well.'

'But why not?'

'We fell out. A long time ago.' She laughed nervously. 'So long ago, I can't even remember why.'

We sat in silence for a moment. Then Mum got up and looked out of the porthole. 'This isn't right; it shouldn't be like this for you,' she murmured as she wiped the porthole with her sleeve.

Then she suddenly twirled round so her skirt flowed out around her. 'I've got it!' she said. 'I know what we'll do.'

'Do? What d'you mean, "do"? I'll just take the note to school, or you could write one, yourself. No one will ever know.'

'Of course they will! No, we can't do that.'

'Yes we can. I'll just –'

'Now Emily, don't start with your arguing. I haven't got the patience for it.' Her mouth tightened into a determined line. 'I cannot allow you to live your life like that.'

'But *you* don't –'

'What I do is my own business,' she snapped. 'Now

please stop answering me back.' She paused for a second before opening her address book. 'No, there's nothing for it. You need to conquer your fear.'

'What are you going to do?' I fiddled with a button on my blouse.

She turned away from me as she picked up the phone. 'I'm going to take you to a hypnotist.'

'All right, Emily. Now, I want you to breathe nice and deeply. Good.'

I was sitting in an armchair in Mystic Millie's back room. I didn't know she did hypnotism but according to Sandra Castle she worked wonders on Charlie Piggot's twitch, and that was good enough for Mum.

'Try to relax,' Millie intoned, before taking a very loud, deep breath. Mum was sitting in a plastic seat in the corner of the room. She wanted to be there, 'just in case'. In case of what, she didn't exactly say.

'You're going to have a little sleep,' Millie drawled. 'When you wake up, your fear of water will have completely gone. Vanished. Floated away . . .'

I had to stay awake! If I fell into a trance and started babbling about everything, the whole plan would be ruined. Not that I had a plan, as such, but you know what I mean. What would Millie think if she found out? What would she do? Visions of nets and cages and scientists' laboratories swam into my mind.

I forced them away.

'Very good,' Millie breathed in a husky voice. 'Now, I'm going to count down from ten to one. As I do, I'd like you to close your eyes and imagine you are on an escalator, gradually travelling down, lower and lower, deeper and deeper. Make yourself as comfortable as you can.'

I shuffled in my seat.

'Ten . . . nine . . . eight . . .' Millie said softly. I closed my eyes and waited nervously for the drowsy feeling to come.

'Seven . . . six . . . five . . .' I pictured myself on an escalator like the one in the precinct in town. I was running the wrong way, scrambling up against the downward motion. I waited.

'Four . . . three . . . two . . . You're feeling very drowsy . . .'

I waited a bit more.

That's when I realised I wasn't feeling drowsy at all. In fact . . .

'One.'

. . . I was wide awake! I'd done it – hooray! Millie *was* a phoney! The 'aura' thing had been a fluke after all!

She didn't say anything for ages and I was starting to get fidgety when a familiar noise broke the silence. I opened my eyes the tiniest crack to see Mum in the opposite corner – fast asleep and snoring like a horse! I snapped my eyes quickly shut again and fought the urge to giggle.

'Now, visualise yourself next to some water,' Millie said in a low voice. 'Think about how you feel about the water. Are you scared? What emotions are you experiencing?'

The only thing I was experiencing was a pain in my side from trying not to laugh.

'And now think of somewhere that you have felt safe. Somewhere you felt happy.' I pictured myself swimming in the sea. I thought about the way my legs became a beautiful tail and about the feeling of zooming along with the fish. I was on the verge of drifting into a happy dream world of my own when – 'Nnnnnuuurrrgggggghhhh!' – Mum let out a huge snore that made me jump out of my chair.

I kept my eyes closed tight and pretended I'd jumped in my sleep. Mum shuffled in her chair and whispered, 'Sorry.'

'Not to worry,' Millie whispered back. 'She's completely under. Just twitching.'

After that, I let my mind drift back to the sea. I couldn't wait to get out there again. Millie's voice carried on in the background and Mum soon started snoring softly again. By the time Millie counted up to seven to wake me up, I was so relieved I hugged her.

'What's that for?' she asked.

'Just a thank you, for curing my fear,' I lied.

She blushed as she slipped Mum's £20 note into her purse. 'Think nothing of it, pet. It's a labour of love.'

Mum was quiet on the way home. Did she know I hadn't been asleep? Did she suspect anything? I didn't dare ask. We made our way through the town's narrow streets down to the prom. As we waited to cross the road, she pointed to a bench facing out to sea. 'Let's go and sit down over there,' she said.

'You OK, Mum?' I asked as casually as I could while we sat on the bench. The tide was out, little pools dotted about in the ripply sand it had left behind.

She peered out towards the horizon. 'I had a dream,' she said without turning round. 'It felt so real. It was beautiful.'

'When? What felt real?'

She looked at me for a second, blinked and turned back to the sea. 'It was out there, somewhere. I can almost feel it.'

'Mum, what are you on about?'

'Promise you won't think I'm crazy.'

'Course I won't.'

She smiled and ruffled my hair. I smoothed it back down. 'When we were at Millie's...' She closed her eyes. 'I dreamed about a shipwreck, under the water. A huge golden boat with a marble mast. A ceiling of amber, a pavement of pearl . . .'

'Huh?'

'It's a line from a poem. I think. I can't remember the rest . . .' She gazed at the sea. 'And the rocks. They weren't like any rocks you've ever seen. They used to glisten every colour you could imagine –'

'*Used* to? What do you mean?'

'Did I say that? I mean they did – in my dream. They shone like a rainbow in water. It's just, it felt so *real*. So familiar...' Her voice trailed away and she gave me a quick sideways look. 'But I suppose it's sometimes like that, isn't it? We all have dreams that feel real. I mean, *you* do. Don't you?'

I was trying to work out what to say when she started waving. 'Oh look,' she said briskly, 'there's Mr Beeston.' I glanced up to see him marching towards the pier. He comes round for afternoon tea every Sunday. Three o'clock on the dot. Mum makes tea; he brings iced buns or doughnuts or caramel slices. I usually scoff mine quickly and leave them to it. I don't know what it is about him. He makes the boat feel smaller, somehow. Darker.

Mum put her fingers in the edges of her mouth and let out a sharp whistle. Mr Beeston turned round. He smiled awkwardly and gave us a quick wave.

Mum stood up. 'Come on. Better get back and put the kettle on.' And before I could ask her anything else, she was marching back to the boat. I had to run to keep up.

28

Chapter Three

I sneaked out again that night. I couldn't keep away. I swam further this time. The sea was grimy with oil and rubbish in the harbour and I wanted to explore the cleaner, deeper water further out.

Looking back across the water, Brightport looked so small. A cluster of buildings all huddled round a tiny horseshoe bay; a lighthouse at one end, a harbour at the other.

A hazy glow hovered over the town. Blurry yellow street lamps with an occasional white light moving along between them.

As I swam round the rocks at the end of the bay, the water became clearer and softer. It was like switching from grainy black and white into colour. The fat grey fish were replaced by stripy yellow and blue ones with floppy silver tails; long thin green ones with spiky antennae and angry mouths; orange ones with spotty black fins – all darting about purposefully around me.

Every now and then, I swam across a shallow sandy stretch. Wispy little stick-like creatures as thin as paper wriggled along beneath me, almost see-through against the sand. Then the water would suddenly get colder and deeper as I went over a rocky bit. I swished myself across these carefully. They were covered in prickly black sea urchins and I didn't fancy getting one of those stuck on my tail.

Soon the water got warmer again as I came to another shallow bit. I was getting tired. I came up for breath and realised I was miles from home; further away than I'd ever been on my own. I tried to flick myself along but my tail flapped lazily and started to ache. Eventually, I made it to a big, smooth rock with a low shelf. I pulled myself out of the water, my tail resting on some pebbles in the sea. A minute later, it went numb. I wiggled my toes and shivered as I watched my legs come back. That bit was still *really* creepy!

Sitting back against a larger rock, I caught my breath. Then I heard something. Like singing, but without words. The wet rocks shimmered in the moonlight but there was no one around. Had I imagined it? The water lapped against the pebbles, making them jangle as it sucked its breath away from the shore. There it was again - the singing.

Where was it coming from? I clambered up a

jagged rock and looked down the other side. That's when I saw her. I rubbed my eyes. Surely it couldn't be . . . but it was! It was a mermaid! A real one! The kind you read about in kids' stories. Long blonde hair all the way down her back, which she was brushing while she sang. She was perched on the edge of a rock, shuffling about as if she was trying to get comfortable. Her tail was longer and thinner than mine. Silvery green and shimmering in the moonlight, it flapped against the rock as she sang.

She kept singing the same song. When she got to the end, she started again. A couple of times, she was in the middle of a really high bit when she stopped and hit her tail with the brush. 'Come on, Shona,' she said sharply. 'Get it right!'

I stared for ages, opening and closing my mouth. Like a fish! I wanted to talk to her. But what exactly do you say to a singing mermaid perched on a rock in the middle of the night? Funnily enough, no one's ever told me.

In the end, I coughed gently and she looked up straight away.

'Oh!' she said. She gawped open-mouthed at my legs for a second. And then with a twist and a splash, she was gone.

I picked my way back down the rocks to the water's edge. 'Wait!' I shouted as she swam away from me. 'I want to talk to you.'

She turned in the water and looked at me suspiciously. 'I'm a mermaid too!' I shouted. Yeah right, with my skinny legs and my Speedo cozzy – she'd *really* believe that! 'Wait, I'll prove it.'

I jumped into the water and started swimming towards her. There was still a moment of panic as my legs stuck together and stiffened. But then they relaxed into their new shape and I relaxed too as I swished my tail and sped through the water.

The mermaid was swimming away from me again. 'Hang on,' I called. 'Watch!' I waited for her to turn back, then dived under and flicked my tail upwards. I waved it as high as I could.

When I came back up, she was staring at me as though she couldn't believe what she'd seen. I smiled but she ducked her head under the water. 'Don't go!' I called. A second later, *her* tail was sticking up. Not twisting around madly like mine did; more as if she was dancing or doing gymnastics. In the moonlight, her tail glinted like diamonds.

When she came back up, I clapped. Tried to anyway, but I slipped back under when I lifted both arms out and got water up my nose.

She was laughing as she swam towards me. 'I haven't seen you before,' she said. 'How old are you?'

'Twelve.'

'Me too. But you're not at my school, are you?'

'Brightport High,' I said. 'Just started.'

'Oh.' She looked worried and moved away from me again.

'What's wrong with that?'

'It's just . . . I haven't heard of it. Is it a mermaid school?'

'You go to a mermaid school?' The idea sounded like something out of a fairy tale, and even though I've *totally* grown out of fairy tales, I had to admit it sounded pretty cool.

She folded her arms – how did she do that without sinking? – and said quite crossly, 'And what's so wrong with that? What kind of school do you *expect* me to go to?'

'No, it sounds great!' I said. 'I wish I did, too.'

I found myself wanting to tell her everything. 'It's just . . . I haven't been a mermaid for long. Or I didn't know I was, or something.' My words jumbled and tumbled out of me. 'I've never really been in water – properly – and then when I did, it happened and I was scared, but I'm not now and I wish I'd found out years ago.'

I looked up to see her staring at me as though I was something from outer space that had got washed up on the beach. I stared back and tried folding my arms, too. I found that if I kept flicking my tail a little, I could stay upright. So I flicked and folded and stared for a bit and she did the same. Then I noticed the side of her mouth flutter a bit and I felt the dimple below my left eye twitching. A second later, we were both laughing like maniacs.

'What are we laughing at?' I said when I managed to catch my breath.

'I don't know!' she answered – and we both burst out laughing again.

'What's your name?' she said once we'd stopped laughing. 'I'm Shona Silkfin.'

'Emily,' I said. 'Emily Windsnap.'

Shona stopped smiling. 'Windsnap? *Really*?'

'Why? What's wrong with that?'

'Nothing – it's just . . .'

'What?'

'No, it's nothing. I thought I'd heard it before but I can't have done. I must be thinking of something else. You haven't been round here before, have you?'

I laughed. 'I'd never even been swimming a couple of weeks ago!'

Shona looked serious for a second. 'How did you do that thing just now?' she asked.

'What thing?'

'With your tail.'

'You mean the handstand? You want me to do it again?'

'No, I mean the other thing.' She pointed under the water. 'How did you make it change?'

'I don't know. It just happens. When I go in water, my legs kind of disappear.'

'I've never seen someone with legs before. Not in real life. I've read about it. What's it like?'

'What's it like having legs?'

Shona nodded.

'Well it's – it's cool. You can walk about, and run. And climb things, or jump or skip.'

Shona gazed at me as if I was talking a foreign language. 'You can't do this with legs,' she said as she dived under again. This time her tail twisted round and round, faster and faster like an upside-down pirouette. Water spun off as she turned, spraying tiny rainbow arcs over the water.

'That was brilliant!' I said when she came back up.

'We've been doing it in Diving and Dance. We're doing a display at the Inter-Bay competition in a couple of weeks. This is the first time I've been in the squad.'

'Diving and dance?'

'Yes,' she went on breathlessly. 'Last year, I was in the choir. Mrs Highwave said that FIVE fishermen were seen wandering aimlessly towards the rocks during my solo performance.' Shona smiled proudly, her earlier shyness totally vanished. 'No one at Shiprock School has *ever* had that many before.'

'And that's – that's good, is it?'

'Good? It's brilliant! I want to be a siren when I grow up.'

I stared at her. 'So all that stuff in fairy tales about mermaids luring fishermen to watery graves – it's all *true*?'

Shona shrugged. 'It's not like we *want* them to die. Not necessarily. Usually, we just hypnotise them into changing their ways and then wipe their memories so they move away and forget they saw us.'

'Wipe their memories?'

'Usually, yes. It's our best defence. Not everyone

knows how to do it. Mainly just sirens and people close to the king. We just use it to stop them stealing all our fish, or finding out about our world.' She leaned in closer. 'Sometimes, they fall in love.'

'The mermaids and the fishermen?'

Shona nodded excitedly. 'There're loads of stories about it. It's *totally* illegal – but so romantic. Don't you think?'

'Well, I guess so. Is that why you were singing just now?'

'Oh, that. No, I was practising for Beauty and Deportment,' she said, as if I had the faintest clue what she was on about. 'We've got a test tomorrow and I can't get my posture right. You have to sit perfectly, tilt your head exactly right and brush your hair in a hundred smooth strokes. It's a pain in the gills trying to remember everything all at once.'

She paused and I guessed it was my turn to say something. 'Mmm, yeah, I know what you mean,' I said, hoping I sounded convincing.

'I came top in last term's test, but that was just hair brushing. This is the lot.'

'That must be difficult.'

'B & D is my favourite subject,' she went on. 'I wanted to be hairbrush monitor but Cynthia Smoothflick got it.' She lowered her voice. 'But Mrs Sharptail told me that if I do well in this test, maybe they'll give it to me next term.'

What was I meant to say to that?

'You think I'm a real goody-goody, don't you?'

She started to swim away again. 'Like everyone else.'

'No, of course not,' I said. 'You're . . . you're . . . ' I struggled to find the right words. 'You're . . . interesting.'

'You're pretty swishy, too,' she said and inched back.

'How come you're out at this time anyway?' I asked.

'These rocks are the best ones around for B & D but you can't really come here in the day. Too dangerous.' She stuck a thumb out towards the coast. 'I usually sneak out on Sunday nights. Or Wednesdays. Mum's always out like a tide by nine o'clock on a Sunday. She likes to be fresh for the week ahead. And she has her aquarobics on Wednesdays and always sleeps more soundly after that. Dad sleeps like a whale every night!' Shona laughed. 'Anyway, I'm glad I came tonight.'

I smiled. 'Me too.' The moon had moved round and was shining down on me, a tiny chink missing from its side. 'But I'll have to get going soon,' I added, yawning.

Shona frowned. 'Are you going to come back another time?'

'Yeah, I'd like that.' She might be a bit strange, but she was a *mermaid!* The only one I'd ever met. She was like me. 'When?'

'Wednesday?'

'Excellent,' I grinned. 'And good luck in your test.'

'Thanks.' And with another flick of her tail, she was gone.

As I swam round Brightport Bay in the darkness, the beam from the lighthouse flashed steady rays across the water. I stopped for a moment to watch. Each beam slowly scanned the water before disappearing round the back of the lighthouse. It was almost hypnotic. A large ship silently made its way across the horizon, a silhouette briefly visible with each slow beam of light.

But then I noticed something else. Someone was standing on the rocks at the bottom of the lighthouse. Mr Beeston! What was he doing? He seemed to be looking out at the horizon – following the ship's progress?

I ducked under the water as another beam came round. What if he'd seen me? I stayed underwater until the light had passed. When I came up again, I looked back at the lighthouse. No one there.

And then the light went off. I waited. It didn't come back on.

I tried to imagine Mr Beeston inside. Just him, all on his own, rattling around in a big empty lighthouse. Footsteps echoing with emptiness whenever he climbed up and down the stone spiral stairs. Sitting alone, looking out at the sea. Watching the light. What kind of a life was that? What kind of a person could live that life? *Why hadn't the light come back on?*

Dark questions followed me home.

By the time I reached the pier, it was nearly morning. Shivering, I pulled myself up the rope ladder.

I sneaked back onto the boat, hung my jacket over the fire. It would be dry by morning. Mum likes the place to be like a sauna at night.

As I crept into bed, I thanked the lucky stars on my ceiling that I'd got home with my secret still safe. For now.

Chapter Four

'*D*on't forget your things.' Mum reached through the side door, holding an object that filled me with dread.

'Right.' I took my swimming bag from her.

'Get a move on, then. You don't want to be late, do you?'

'No. Course not.' I looked down at the rippled sand between the wooden slats of the jetty. 'Mum?' I said quietly.

'What, sweetheart?'

'Do I have to go to school?'

'Have to go? Of course you have to go. What cock-eyed notions have you got in your head now?'

'I don't feel well.' I clutched my tummy and tried to look as if I was in pain.

Mum pulled herself through the door and

crouched on the jetty in front of me. She cupped my chin in her hand and lifted my face up to look at hers. I *hate* it when she does that. The only way I can avoid her eyes is by closing my own, and then I feel like an idiot.

'What's this about?' she asked. 'Is it your new school? Don't you like it?'

'School's fine,' I said quickly. 'On the whole.'

'What, then? Is it the swimming?'

I tried to move my head away but she held on tight. 'No,' I lied, looking as far to the side as I could, my head still trapped in her hand.

'I thought we had that all fixed,' she said. 'Are you worried in case it hasn't worked?'

Now, why hadn't I thought of that? How could I have been so stupid! I should have realised that if I was cured I'd have to go swimming again!

'I've got a bad stomach,' I said weakly.

Mum let go of my chin. 'Come on, sausage, there's nothing wrong with you, and you know it. Now, scoot.' She patted my leg and stood up. 'You'll be fine,' she added, more gently.

'Hm,' I replied, and sloped up the jetty to wait for the bus on the promenade.

I slunk into school and got to my class just as Mrs Partington was closing the registration book. She looked at her watch and said, 'I'll turn a blind eye, just this once.'

She always says that. Everyone laughs when she does because she actually has got a blind eye. It's bright blue, just like her other one, but it doesn't move. Just stares at you, even when she's looking away. Freaky. You don't know where to look when she's talking to you, so we all try not to get told off. She always has the best-behaved class in the school.

I didn't laugh with the others this time, though. Just said, 'Sorry,' and went to sit down, pushing my hateful bag under the table.

The morning was a disaster. I couldn't concentrate at all. We were doing long division and I kept putting the numbers in the wrong place. I was really cross because I can do long division *easily*. Mrs Partington kept giving me sideways looks out of her good eye.

When the bell rang for break, I actually did start to feel ill. We had to line up for the coach to take us to the baths. Everyone ran out of the room but I took ages putting my pens and ruler away in my pencil case.

Mrs Partington was wiping the board. 'Come on, Emily,' she said without turning round. 'It might be nice to get to *something* on time today.'

'Yes, Mrs Partington,' I said and crawled out of the classroom, reluctantly dragging my bag behind me.

I walked to the coach like a zombie. It crossed my mind just to keep walking and not get on the coach at all. I'd got as far as the school gate when Philip Northwood called me back. 'Oi – teacher's pet!' he yelled. Everyone turned to see who he was talking to.

'Teacher's pet? What are you on about?'

'Come on, we all saw you showing off last week in the pool. Bob couldn't stop going on about how *amazing* you were and how we should all try and be like *you*.'

'Yeah. We all heard what he said.' Mandy Rushton came up behind Philip. 'And we *saw* you.'

I glared at her, speechless. She saw me? Saw *what*? My tail? She couldn't have! It hadn't even formed – *had it*?

'I can't help it,' I said, eventually.

'Yeah, right. *Show-off*,' Mandy sneered.

'Shut up.'

Mr Bird, the PE teacher, turned up then. 'Right, come on, you lot,' he said. 'Let's have you all on this coach.'

I found a seat on my own. Julie sat across the aisle from me. 'He's such a pig, that Philip,' she said, putting her bag on her knee. I smiled at her. 'And he's only jealous because he doesn't know how to swim.'

'Thanks Ju–'

'Shift up, Jules.' Mandy plonked herself down next to Julie and flashed me a smarmy smile. 'Unless you want to sit with *fish girl*.'

Julie went red and I turned to look out of the window as the coach bumped and bounced down the road. Mandy's words swirled round and round in my head as if they were in a cement mixer. *Fish girl*? What did she mean?

The coach stopped in the car park. 'You coming?' Julie hung back while Mandy pushed and shoved to the front with the rest.

'Won't be a sec.' I pretended to be doing up my shoelaces. Perhaps I could hide under the seat till everyone came back, say I'd fainted or fallen over or something.

I could hear chattering outside the window, then it went quiet. A moment later, there was a huge groan, people shouting.

'But *sir*, that's not *fair*,' I heard Philip whine. I chanced a quick look out of the window. Bob was there, talking to Mr Bird. The class were all standing around; some had thrown their bags on the ground.

Next thing I knew, someone had got on the coach. I ducked down again, held my breath. But the footsteps came all the way to the back.

'You're not still doing your laces up, are you?' It was Julie.

'Huh?' I looked up.

'What are you doing?'

'I'm just –'

'Doesn't matter anyway.' She sat down. 'Swimming's off.'

'*What?*'

'Staff are on strike. Council cuts. They forgot to tell the school.'

'You're joking?'

'Do I look as though I'm joking?'

I looked at her face; totally miserable. I stared down at my lap and shook my head. 'God, it's just not fair, is it?' I said, trying hard not to grin. 'Wonder what they'll make us do instead.'

'That's what Mr Bird's talking about now with Bob. They're going to send us on a nature trail, apparently.'

'Duh – boring,' I folded my arms, hoping I looked in as much of a huff as Julie. The coach soon set off again and Mr Bird announced with a smile that we were going to Macefin Wood.

Mandy glared at me as she sat down across the aisle. I had to sit on my hands to stop myself punching the air and shouting, 'Ye-e-e-s!'

I went to bed really early so I could get a few hours' sleep before sneaking out to meet Shona. I found my way to the rocks easily and got there first this time. A familiar flick of a tail spreading rainbow droplets over the water told me she'd arrived.

'Hello!' I waved as soon as she surfaced.

'Hi!' She waved back. 'Come on.'

'Where are we going?'

'You'll see.' She splashed rainbow water in my face with her tail as she dived under.

We seemed to swim for ages. The water reminded me of those adverts where they pour a load of melted chocolate into the bar. Silky smooth. I felt as if I was melting with it as we swam.

Shona was ahead of me, gliding through the water and glancing back from time to time to check I was still there. Every now and then, she'd point to the left or right. I'd follow her hand to see a hundred tiny fish swimming in formation like a gymnastics display, or a yellow piece of seaweed climbing up towards the surface like a sunflower. A line of grey fish swam alongside us for a while; fast, smart and pinstriped like city businessmen.

It was only when we stopped and came up for air that I realised we'd been swimming underwater the whole time.

'How did I do that?' I gasped, breathless.

'Do what?' Shona looked puzzled.

I looked back at the rocks. They were tiny pebbles in the distance. 'We must have swum a mile.'

'Mile and a quarter, actually.' Shona looked apologetic. 'My dad bought me a splishometer for my last birthday.'

'A *what*?'

'Sorry. I keep forgetting you've not been a mermaid very long. It shows how far you've swum. I measured the distance from Rainbow Rocks yesterday.'

'Rainbow what?'

'You know. Where we met.'

'Oh, right.' I suddenly realised I was out of my depth – in more ways than one.

'I wasn't sure if it would be too far for you but I wanted to bring you here.'

I looked round. Sea everywhere. What was so special about this particular spot? 'Why here?' I asked. 'And anyway, you haven't answered my question. How did we do all that underwater?'

Shona shrugged. 'We're mermaids,' she said simply. 'Come on, I want to show you something.' And with that, she disappeared again and I dived under the water after her.

The lower we went, the colder the water grew. Fish flashed by in the darkness.

A huge grey bruiser with black dots slid slowly past, its mouth slightly open in a moody frown. Pink jellyfish danced and trampolined around us.

'Look.' Shona pointed to our left as a slow-motion tornado of thin black fish came towards us, whirling and spiralling as it passed us by.

I shivered as we swam deeper still. Eventually, Shona grabbed my hand and pointed down. All I could see was what looked like the biggest rug I'd ever seen in my life – made out of seaweed!

'What's that? I gurgled.

'I'll show you.' And with that, Shona pulled me lower. Seaweed slipped and slid along my body, creaking and popping as we swam through it. What was she *doing* with me? Where was she taking me?

I was about to say I'd had enough, but then the weeds became thinner. It was as though we'd been stuck in a wood and finally made our way out. Or to a clearing in the centre of it, anyway. We'd come to a patch of sand in the middle of the seaweed forest.

'What is it?' I asked.

'What d'you think?'

I looked around me. A huge steel tube lay along the ground; next to it, metres of fishing nets sprawled across the sand, reaching up into the weeds. A couple of old bicycles were propped up on huge rusty springs. 'I have absolutely no idea,' I said.

'It's our playground. We're not really meant to come out here. But everyone does.'

'Why can't you come here?'

'You're meant to stick to your own area – it's too dangerous otherwise. Too easy to get spotted.' Shona swam over to the tube and disappeared. 'Come on,' her voice bubbled out from inside it, echoing spook-ily around the clearing.

I followed her into the tube, sliding along the cold steel to the other end. By the time I came out, Shona was already flipping herself up the fishing net. I scrambled up behind her.

'Like it?' Shona asked when we came back down.

'Yeah, it's wicked.'

Shona looked at me blankly. 'It's wicked?'

'Wicked . . . cool, top. You know –'

'You mean like swishy?'

'I guess so.' I looked around me. 'Where's all this stuff from?'

'Things fall into the sea – or get thrown away. We make use of it,' she said as she pulled herself onto one

48

of the bikes. She perched sideways on it, letting herself sway backwards and forwards as the spring swung to and fro. 'Nice to have someone to share it with,' she added.

I looped my tail over the other one and turned to face her. 'How d'you mean? What about your friends?'

'Well, I've got *friends*. Just not a *best* friend. I think the others think I'm too busy swotting to be anyone's best friend.'

'Well, you do seem to work pretty hard,' I said. 'I mean, sneaking out at night to revise for a test!'

'Yeah, I know. Do you think I'm really dull?'

'Not at all! I think you're . . . I think you're swishy!'

Shona smiled shyly.

'How come there's no one else around?' I asked. 'It's kind of creepy.'

'It's the middle of the night, gill-brain!'

'Oh yeah. Of course.' I held onto the handlebars as I swayed forwards and back on my swing. 'I wish I could meet some other mermaids,' I said after a while.

'Why don't you, then? You could come to my school!'

'How? You don't have extra lessons in the middle of the night, do you?'

'Come in the day. Come on Saturday.'

'*Saturday?*'

'We have school Saturday mornings. Why not come with me this Saturday? I'll tell them you're my long-lost cousin. It'd be evil.'

'Evil?'

'Wicked. Sorry.'

I thought about it. I'd been invited to Julie's on Saturday. I could easily tell Mum I was going there and then tell Julie I couldn't make it. But I was only just getting to know Julie – she might not ask me again. *Then* who would I have? Apart from Shona! And Shona *was* a mermaid. She was going to take me to mermaid school! When else would I get a chance to do *that*?

'OK,' I said. 'Let's do it!'

'Great! Will your parents mind?'

'You're joking aren't you? No one knows about me being a mermaid.'

'You mean apart from your mum and dad? If you're a mermaid, they must be –'

'I haven't got a dad,' I said.

'Oh. Sorry.'

'It's OK. I never had one. He left us when I was a baby.'

'Sharks! How awful.'

'Yeah, well, I don't want to know about him anyway. He never even said he was leaving, you know. Just disappeared. Mum's never got over it.'

Shona didn't reply. She'd gone all rigid and was staring at me.

'What?'

'Your dad left when you were a baby?'

'Yes.'

'And you don't know why he went?'

I shook my head.

'Or where?'

'Nope. But after what he did to Mum, he can stay there as far as I'm –'

'But what if something happened to him?'

'Like what?'

'Like – like – maybe he got taken away, or he couldn't come back to you or something.'

'He left us. And we're fine without him.'

'But what if he didn't –'

'Shona! I don't want to talk about it. I haven't got a dad, OK? End of subject.' I watched a shoal of long white fish swim across the clearing and disappear into the weeds. Seaweed swayed gently behind them.

'Sorry,' Shona said. 'Are you still going to come on Saturday?'

I pulled a face. 'If you still want me to.'

'Of course I do!' She swung off her bike. 'Come on. We need to be heading back.'

We swam silently back to Rainbow Rocks, my head filled with sadness stirred up by Shona's questions. Not so different from the ones I'd asked myself a hundred times. Why *did* my dad disappear? Didn't he love me? Didn't he want me? Was it my fault?

Would I ever, *ever* see him?

Chapter Five

I waved to Mum as I made my way down the pier. 'Bye darling, have a lovely day,' she called.

Go back in, go back in, I thought. 'Bye,' I smiled back at her. I walked woodenly along the pier, glancing behind me every few seconds. She was smiling and waving every time I looked.

Eventually, she went inside and closed the side door behind her. I carried on to the top of the pier, checked behind me one last time, just to be sure – then, instead of turning onto the promenade, I ran down the steps onto the beach and sneaked under the pier. I pulled off my jeans and shoes and shoved them under a rock. I already had my cozzy on underneath.

The tide was in so I only had to creep a short way under the pier. A few people were milling about on the beach, but no one looked my way. What if they did? For a second, I pictured them all pointing at me: 'Fish girl! Fish girl!' Laughing; chasing me with a net.

I couldn't do it!

But Shona! And mermaid school! I *had* to do it. I'd swim underwater all the way to Rainbow Rocks. No one would see my tail.

Before I could change my mind, I ran into the freezing cold water. One last look round, then I took a breath, dived forward – and was on my way.

I made my way to Rainbow Rocks and hung around at the edge of the water, keeping hidden from the shore. A minute later, Shona arrived.

'You're here!' she grinned and we dived under. She took me in a new direction, out across Shiprock Bay. When we came to the furthest tip of the bay, Shona turned to me. 'Are you ready for this?' she asked.

'Are you joking? I can't wait!'

She flipped herself over and started swimming downwards. I copied her moves, scaling the rocks as we dived deeper and deeper.

Shoals of fish darted out from gaps in rocks that I hadn't even noticed. Sea urchins clung to the sides in thick black crowds. The water grew colder.

And then Shona disappeared.

I flicked my tail and sped down. There was a gap in

the rock. A huge hole, in fact. Big enough for a whale to get through! Shona's face appeared from inside.

'Come on,' she grinned.

'Into the rock?'

She swam back out and grabbed my hand. We went through together. It was a dark tunnel, bending and twisting. Eventually, we turned a corner and a glimmer of light appeared, growing bigger and bigger until eventually we came out of the tunnel. I stared around me, my jaw wide open.

We were in a massive hole in the rock. It must have been the size of a football pitch. Bigger! Tunnels and caves led off in all directions, around the edges, above us, below. A giant underwater rabbit warren!

Everywhere I looked, people were swimming this way and that. And they all had tails! Merpeople! Hundreds of them! There were mermaids with gold chains round slinky long tails, swimming along with little merchildren. One had a merbaby on her back, the tiniest little pink tail sticking out from under its sling. A group of mermaids huddled outside one passageway, talking and laughing together, bags made from fishing nets on their arms. Three old mermen sat outside another, their tails faded and wrinkled, their faces full of lines and their eyes sparkling as they talked and laughed.

'Welcome to Shiprock – merfolk style!' Shona said.

'Come on, Shona. Don't want to be late.' A

mermaid with her hair in a tall bun appeared beside us. 'Five minutes to the bell.' Then she flicked her dark green tail and zoomed off ahead.

'That's Mrs Tailspin,' Shona said. 'History teacher. We've got her first thing.'

We followed her along a tube-like channel in the rock. At the other end, where it opened up again, mergirls and boys were swimming together in groups, swishing tails in a hundred different shades of blue and green and purple and silver as they milled about, waiting for school to start. A group of girls were playing a kind of skipping game with a long piece of ship's rope.

Then a noise like a foghorn surrounded us. Everyone suddenly swam into lines. Boys on one side, girls on another. Shona pulled me along to a line at the far end. 'You OK?'

I nodded, still unable to speak as we filed down yet another tunnel with the rest of our line.

We each took our seats on smooth round rocks dotted about the circular room. It reminded me of the 360 degree dome at the fair where they show films of daredevil flights and crazy downhill skiing. Only this wasn't a film – it was real!

Shona grabbed an extra rock and pulled it next to hers. A few of the other girls smiled at me.

'Are you new?' one asked. She was little and plump with a thick, dark green tail. It shimmered and sparkled as she spoke.

'She's my cousin,' Shona answered quickly. The

girl smiled and went to sit on her rock.

The walls were covered with collages made from shells and seaweed. Light filtered in through tiny cracks in the ceiling. Then Mrs Tailspin came in and we all jumped off our rocks to say good morning.

Shona put her hand up straight away. 'Is it all right if my cousin sits in with us, please miss?'

Mrs Tailspin looked me up and down. 'If she's good.'

Then she clapped her hands. 'Right, let's get started. Shipwrecks. Today, we're doing the nineteenth century.'

Shipwrecks! That beats long division!

Mrs Tailspin passed various objects around the room. 'These are all from *The Voyager*,' she said as she passed a huge plank of wood to a girl at the front. 'One of our proudest sinkings.'

Proudest sinkings – what did *that* mean?

'Not a huge amount is known for sure about *The Voyager*, but what we do know is that a group of mermaids who called themselves the Siren Sisters were responsible for its great sinking. Through skilful manipulation and careful luring, they managed to distract the entire crew for long enough to bring the great ship down.'

Shona passed me a couple of interlocked pieces of chain. I examined them and passed them on.

'Now, the only problem with this sinking was the actions of one or two of the Siren Sisters. Can anyone think what they might have done?'

56

Shona thrust her hand in the air.

'Yes, Shona?'

'Miss, did they fall in love?'

'Now, how did I know you were going to say that? Ever the romantic, aren't you Shona?'

A giggle went round the room.

'Well, as a matter of fact, Shona is right,' Mrs Tailspin went on. 'Some of these sisters let down the entire operation. Instead of dispersing the crew, they chose to run away with them! Never to be seen again. It's not known whether they attempted to return once they discovered the inevitable disappointments of life ashore . . .'

I shuffled uncomfortably on my rock.

'. . . although as you know,' Mrs Tailspin continued, 'Neptune takes a *very* dim view of those who do.'

'Who's Neptune?' I whispered to Shona.

'The king,' she whispered back. 'And you don't want to get on the wrong side of him, believe me! He's got a terrible temper – he makes thunderstorms and all sorts when he gets in a bad mood. Or unleashes sea monsters! But he can calm the roughest seas with a blink. *Very* powerful. And *very* rich, too. Lives in this huge palace, all made of coral and gems and gold –'

'Shona, are you talking?' Mrs Tailspin was looking our way.

'Sorry, miss.' Shona blushed.

Mrs Tailspin shook her head. 'Now, one rather

sorry piece of *The Voyager*'s legacy,' she went on, 'is that it has become somewhat of a symbol for those who choose to follow their Siren Sisters' doomed path. Instances are rare, but merfolk and humans *have* been caught together here. I needn't tell you that the punishments have been harsh. Our prison is home to a number of those traitors who have attempted to endanger our population in this way.'

'You have a prison?' I whispered.

'Of course,' Shona replied. 'Really scary, from the pictures I've seen. A huge labyrinth of caves out beyond the Great Mermer Reef, near Neptune's palace.'

I couldn't concentrate for the rest of the morning. What if they found out I wasn't a real mermaid and *I* ended up in that prison?

Shona grabbed me as soon as lessons finished.

'I've had an amazing thought,' she said. 'Let's go to the shipwreck. Let's find it!'

'What? How?'

'Mrs Tailspin told us the exact location.'

She ran her hand along the side of her tail. Then she did this totally weird thing. Put her hand inside her scales. Felt around for a bit, then pulled something out of them! It looked like a cross between a compass and a calculator. Her scales closed up as she pulled her hand out.

'What was *that*?' I screeched.

'What?' Shona looked baffled.

I pointed to her tail, where her hand had disappeared.

58

'My pocket?'

'*Pocket?*'

'Course. You have pockets.'

'In my denim jacket, yeah. Not in my *body*.'

'Really? Are you sure?'

I fumbled round the sides of my tail. My hand slipped through a gap. Pockets! I did have them!

Shona held up the object she'd pulled out. 'We'll find the shipwreck with my splishometer.'

Mum wasn't expecting me home till four o' clock. Should we?

'Come on Emily; it must be *such* a romantic place!'

I thought for a second. 'OK, let's do it – let's go this afternoon!'

We made our way slowly out to sea, Shona checking her splishometer every few metres. After a while, we came up to the surface to look around. A lone line of seagulls skimmed the surface. Ahead of us, seabirds like white arrows shot into the water.

We ducked under again. Rays of sun shone in dusty beams under the water. Moments later, Shona's splishometer beeped. 'We're getting close,' she breathed as we dived lower.

As we swam deeper, the sea life became weirder. Something that looked like a peach with tentacles turned slowly round in the water, scanning its surroundings with beady black eyes. Further down, a see-through jellyfish bounced away from us - a slow motion space hopper. A rubbery gold crown floated silently upwards. Everywhere I looked, fish that could have passed for cartoon aliens bounced and twirled and spun.

Shona grabbed my arm. 'Come on,' she said, pointing ahead and swimming away again. Lower and lower, the sea grew darker and darker. As we pressed forward, something came into view. I couldn't make out the shape but it was surrounded by a hazy, golden light. The light grew stronger as we carried on swimming towards it; and bigger. It was everywhere, all around us. We'd found it! *The Voyager!*

We darted along its length, tracing the row of portholes all the way from the back end to its pointy front, then swam away again to take it all in. Long and sleek, the ship lay on a tilt in the sand: still, silent, majestic.

'That is so-o-o amazing.' My words gurgled away from me like a speech bubble in a comic strip. It made me laugh, which sent more bubbles floating out of my mouth, up into the darkness.

I couldn't stop staring at the ship. It was like something out of a film – not real life. *My* life! It shone as if it had the sun inside it, as though it was made of gold.

Made of gold? A shipwreck made of gold? A queasy feeling clutched at my insides.

'Shona, the masts –'

'You OK?' Shona asked.

'I need to see a mast!'

Shona pointed up into the darkness again. 'Come on.'

Neither of us spoke as we skirted round the hundreds of tiny fish pecking away at its sides, and up to the deck. Metre after metre of wooden slats: some shiny, almost new looking, others dark and rotting. We swam upwards, circled one of the masts, wrapping our tails round it like snakes slithering up a tree, my heart hammering loud and fast.

'What is it?'

'What?'

'What's it made of?'

Shona moved back to examine the mast. 'Well, it looks like marble, but that's –'

'Marble? Are you sure?'

A golden boat with a marble mast. No!

I let go of the mast and pushed myself away, scattering a shoal of blue fish as I raced back down to the hull. I had to get away! It wasn't right! It didn't make sense!

'What's wrong?' Shona was behind me.

'It's – it's –' *What?* What could I say? How could I explain this awful panic inside me? It didn't make sense. I was being ridiculous. It *couldn't* be – of course it couldn't! I pushed the thought from my mind. Just a coincidence.

'It's nothing,' I said, laughing off my unease. 'Come on, let's go inside!'

61

Shona slithered along the hull. Fish nibbled at its sides next to her. I shivered as a silky plant brushed against my arm, swaying with the motion of the sea.

'Found one!' She flapped her tail excitedly.

I slithered over to join her and found myself in front of a broken porthole.

She looked at me for a second, her bright face reflecting the boat's light. 'I've never had a real adventure before,' she said quietly. Then she disappeared through the empty window. I forced the fear out of my mind. There was nothing to be afraid of. Then I held my arms tight against my sides, flicked the end of my tail and followed Shona through the porthole.

We were in a narrow corridor. Bits of wallpaper dripped from the ceiling in watery stalactites, swaying with the movement of the sea. Below us, the slanted floor was completely rotten: black and mouldy with the odd floorboard missing. The walls were lined with plankton.

'Come on.' Shona led the way. Long thin fish silently skirted the walls and ceiling. Portholes lined the corridor on our left; doors with paint peeling and cracking all the way down faced them on our right. We tried every one.

'They're all locked,' Shona said, wiggling another rotting doorknob and pushing her weight against another stubborn door. Then she raced ahead to the end of the corridor and disappeared. I followed her round the corner. Right in front of our eyes, a white door seemed to be challenging us. It was bigger than the others, shining and glowing, its brass round handle begging to be turned. A big fat fish hovered in front of it, beady-eyed like a goalkeeper. Shona tossed her head as she leant forward to try the handle, her hair flowing out in the water. The fish darted away.

The door swung open.

'Swishing heck!' she breathed.

I joined her in the doorway. 'Wow!' Bubbles danced out of my mouth as I stared.

It was the grandest room I'd ever seen – and the biggest! Easily as big as a tennis court. At one end, carpet made out of maroon weeds swayed gently with the sea's rhythm. At the other, a hard white floor.

'Pearl,' Shona said, gliding across its shiny surface.

I swam into a corner and circled one of the golden pillars shining bright light across the room. With every movement, rainbow colours flickered around the walls and ceiling. Bright blue and yellow fish danced in the light.

Below huge round windows, benches with velvet seats and high wooden backs lined the walls, large iron tables dotted about in front of them. I picked up a goblet from one of the tables. Golden and heavy, its base was a long skirt, the cup a deep well waiting to be filled with magic.

Above us, a shoal of fish writhed and spun along the yellow ceiling. The ceiling!

'Shona, what's the ceiling made out of?'

She swam up to its surface. 'Amber, by the looks of it.'

I backed out of the room, flicking my tail as hard as I could. *A ceiling of amber, a pavement of pearl.* No! It couldn't be! It was impossible!

But I couldn't brush the truth away this time.

It was the boat from Mum's dream.

Chapter Six

'*S*hona, we've got to get out of here!' I pulled at her hand. My fingers shook.

'But don't you want to –'

'We have to get away!'

'What is it?'

'I don't know. Something's not right. *Please,* Shona.'

She looked at my face and for a moment I saw shock – or recognition. 'Come on,' she said.

We didn't speak as we slithered back down the narrow corridor in silence, Shona following as I raced ahead. I swam back in such a panic I went straight past the broken porthole and almost all the way to the other end of the boat! I turned and was about to start swimming back when Shona tugged at my arm.

'Look,' she said, pointing at the floor.

'What?'

'Can't you see?'

I looked closer and noticed a shiny section of wood, newer than the other floorboards, the size of a manhole. It had a handle on it shaped like a giant pair of pliers.

Shona pulled at the trapdoor. 'Give me a hand.'

'Shona, I've got a really weird feeling about all this. I have to – '

'Just a quick look. *Please*. Then we'll go – I promise.'

Reluctantly, I pulled at the handle with her, flipping my tail to propel myself backwards. Seconds later, it creaked open. A swarm of tiny fish darted out from the gap, shimmering in a flash of silver before disappearing down the corridor.

Shona flipped herself upside down and poked her head into the hole, swishing her tail in my face. 'What can you see?' I asked.

'It's a tunnel!' Shona flipped back up and grabbed my hand. 'Have a look.'

'But you said we could – '

'*Five* minutes.' And she disappeared down the hole.

As soon as we got into the tunnel, the golden light virtually disappeared. Just tiny rays peeping through the odd crack. We felt our way along the sides – which wasn't exactly pleasant. Slimy, rubbery things lined the walls. I decided not to think about what they might be. An occasional fish passed by in the shadows: slow and solitary. The silence seemed to deepen. Inside it, my unease grew and grew. *How could it be? How could it?*

'Look!' Shona's voice echoed in front of me.

I peered ahead. We'd reached another door, facing us at the end of the tunnel. 'Locked,' Shona said quietly. 'Hey, but look at – '

Suddenly a luminous fish with a huge wide-open jaw sprang out of the darkness, almost swimming into my face.

I screamed and grabbed Shona's arm. 'I'm getting out of here!' I burst out, forgetting about the ballroom, the slimy rubbery walls, the trapdoor. All that mattered was getting away from that ship.

We sat on Rainbow Rocks, low down by the water's edge, out of sight from the coast. Water lapped gently against the stones. Shona's tail glistened in the chilly light. Mine had disappeared again and I rubbed my goosepimply legs dry with my jacket. Shona stared. She obviously found the transformation as weird as I did!

'Do you want to tell me what this is about?' She broke the silence.

'What?'

'What happened to you back there?'

I threw a pebble into the water and watched the circle around it grow bigger and wider until it disappeared. 'I can't.'

'Don't want to?'

'No, I mean I really, actually can't! I don't even know what it's about, myself.'

Shona fell quiet again. 'I understand if you don't trust me,' she said after a while. 'I mean, it's not as if I'm your best friend or anything.'

'I haven't got a best friend at the moment.'

'Like me.' Shona smiled shyly, her tail flapping on the rock as she spoke.

Then we fell quiet again. 'Look, it's not that I don't trust you,' I said after a while. 'I do. It's just . . . you might think I'm mad.'

'Course I won't. Apart from the fact that you're a human half the time and a mermaid who sneaks out to play at night, I haven't met anyone as normal as you in ages!'

I smiled.

'Try me,' she said.

So I did. I told her everything; I told her about the swimming lesson and Mystic Millie and about Mum's dream and the ship being exactly the same. I even told her about seeing Mr Beeston on my way home that first night. Once I'd started, I couldn't seem to stop.

When I'd finished, Shona stared at me without speaking.

'What?'

She looked away.

'*What?*'

'I don't want to say. You might get cross, like last time.'

'What d'you mean? Do you know something? You've *got* to tell me.'

Shona shook her head. 'I don't know anything, not for sure.'

'What is it? *Tell* me.'

'You remember when we first met, and I thought I'd heard your name before?'

'You said you'd got it wrong.'

'I know. But I don't think I had.'

'You *had* heard it?'

She nodded. 'I think so.'

'Where?'

'It was at school.'

'At *school*?'

'I think it was in a book. I never knew if it was true, or just an ocean-myth. We did it in history.'

'Did *what* in history?'

Shona paused before saying in a quiet voice, 'Illegal marriages.'

'Illegal? You mean –'

'Between merpeople and humans.'

I tried to take her words in. What did she mean? What was she trying to tell me? That my parents –

'There'll be something at the library in school. Let's go back.' Shona slid down off her rock.

'I thought school finished at lunch time.'

'There are clubs and societies in the afternoon. Come on, I'm sure we can find out more.'

I slipped into the water and followed her back to mermaid school, my thoughts as tangled as a heap of washed up fishing nets.

Back through the hole in the rock; back along the caves and tunnels and tubes until we came to the school playground. It was empty.

'This way.' Shona pointed to a rocky structure standing on its own. Spiral-shaped and full of giant holes and crevices. We swam inside through a thick crack and slithered up through the swirls, coming out into a circular room with jagged rocky edges. A few mergirls and boys sat on mushroom-shaped spongy seats in front of long pieces of scratchy paper that hung from the ceiling. They wound the paper up or down, silently moving their heads from side to side as they examined the sheets.

'What are they doing?' I whispered.

Shona gawped at me. 'Reading! What d'you think they're doing?'

I shrugged. 'Where are the books?'

'It's easier to find stuff on scrolls. Everything's

stored here. Come on.' She led me to the opposite side of the room and swam up to the ceiling. We looked through different headings at the top of each scroll: *Shipwrecks, Treasures, Fishermen, Sirens.*

'Sirens – it might be this one,' Shona said, pulling on the end of a thick roll. 'Give me a hand.'

We pulled the scroll down to the floor, hooked it in place on a roller, then wound an old wooden handle round and round, working our way through facts and figures, dates and events. Stories about mermaids luring fishermen into the ocean with songs so beautiful they were almost impossible to hear; of fishermen going mad, throwing themselves into the sea to follow their hearts' desires; mermaids winning praise and riches for their success; ships brought down. We searched the whole scroll. Nothing about illegal marriages.

'We'll never find anything,' I said. 'I don't even know what we're looking for.'

Shona was swimming around above me. 'There must be something,' she muttered.

'Why is it so illegal, anyway? Why can't people marry who they want?'

'It's the one thing that makes Neptune *really* angry. Some say it's because he once married a human and then she left him.'

'Neptune's married?' I swam up to join her.

'Oh, he's got loads of wives, and hundreds of children! But this one was special, and he's never forgiven her – or the rest of the human race!'

'Shona Silkfin – what are you doing here?' A voice boomed from behind us. We both spun round to see someone swimming towards us. The history teacher!

'Oh, Mrs Tailspin. I was just, we were –'

'Shona was just trying to help me with my homework,' I said with an innocent smile.

'Homework?' Mrs Tailspin looked at us doubtfully.

'At my school, in – in –'

'Shallowpool,' Shona said quickly. 'That's where my cousin's from.'

'And we've got to do a project on illegal marriages,' I continued as an idea came to me. Maybe she'd know something! After all, Shona did say she heard my name in a history lesson. 'Shona said that she'd studied them. She was trying to help me.'

Mrs Tailspin swam down to a mushroomy sponge-seat and beckoned us to do the same. 'What do you want to know?'

I paused, glancing at Shona. What *did* I want to know? Did I want to know at all?

'Emily's doing her project on Shiprock,' Shona said, picking up my thread. 'That's why she's here. We needed to find out if there had been any round here.'

'Indeed there has been one,' Mrs Tailspin said, patting the bun on her head. 'Rather a well-known incident. Do you remember, Shona? We covered it last term.' She frowned. 'Or were you too busy chatting at the time?'

'Can you tell me about it?' I asked.

72

Mrs Tailspin turned back to me. 'Very well.'

I tried to keep still on my sponge while I waited for her to carry on.

'A group of humans once found out a little too much about the merfolk world,' she began. 'There'd been a yacht race nearby. A couple of the boats went off course and capsized. Some mermen found them and helped them. They had to have their memories wiped afterwards.' She paused. 'But one was missed.'

'And?'

'And she didn't forget. Word spread, both in her world and our own. They started meeting up. Humans and merfolk. At one point, there was talk of them all going off to a desert island to live together. The rumour was that there was even a place where it was already happening.'

'*Really*?' Shona said.

'Like I said, it was a rumour. I don't believe for one moment that it exists. But they kept meeting. As I'm sure you can imagine, Neptune was *not* pleased.'

'What happened?' I asked.

'There were storms for weeks. He said that if he caught anyone, they would be imprisoned for life. He visited every merfolk area personally.'

'He hardly ever does that!' Shona said. 'He always stays in his palace, except when he goes on exotic holidays, or visits his other palaces. He's got them all over the world, hasn't he?'

'That's right, Shona.'

'So he came to Shiprock?' I asked.

'He did indeed.'

Shona bounced off her seat. 'Did you meet him?'

Mrs Tailspin nodded.

'Really? What's he like?'

'Angry, loud, covered in gold – but with a certain charisma.'

'Wow!' Shona gazed at Mrs Tailspin.

'The preparation took weeks,' she continued. 'As you know, Neptune can become most unhappy if he is not presented with adequate jewels and crystals when he visits. Our menfolk went on daily searches under the rocks. We made him a new sceptre as a present.'

'Was he pleased?'

'Very. He gave the town a dolphin as a thank you.'

'So, did the meetings stop?' I asked. 'Between the merpeople and the humans?'

'Sadly, no. They continued to meet in secret. I don't know how they lived with themselves, defying Neptune like that.'

'And the marriage...?' I asked, holding my breath.

'Yes, there was a merman. A poet. Jake. He married one of the women, at Rainbow Rocks –'

Something stirred in the back of my mind; thoughts that I couldn't quite grasp, like bubbles that burst as soon as you touch them.

Shona didn't look at me. 'What was his last name?' she asked, her voice jagged like the library walls.

Mrs Tailspin patted her bun again. Tutted. Squinted. 'Whirlstand? Whichmap? Wisplatch? No, I can't remember.'

Looking down, I closed my eyes. 'Was it Wind-snap?' I asked.

'Windsnap! Yes, that might have been it.'

The bubbles turned to rocks and started clogging up my throat.

'And they had a daughter,' she continued. 'That was when they were caught.'

'When exactly was this?' I managed to squeeze out.

'Let's see...twelve or thirteen years ago.'

I nodded, not trusting myself to speak.

'Gave themselves away with that. The silly woman brought the child to Rainbow Rocks and that was when we got him.'

'*Got* him? What did they do to him?' Shona asked.

'Prison,' Mrs Tailspin said with a proud smile. 'Neptune decided to make an example of him. He said Jake would be locked up for life.'

'What about the baby?' I asked, swallowing hard while I waited for her to reply.

'Baby? Goodness knows. But we stopped that one.' Mrs Tailspin smiled again. 'That's what you'll be doing when you're a siren, Shona. You'll be as good as that.'

Shona reddened. 'I haven't completely decided what I want to be yet,' she said.

'Very well.' Mrs Tailspin glanced round the room. Mergirls and boys were still reading. Some were talking quietly in groups. 'Now, girls, if there's nothing else, I must check on my library group.'

'Yes. Thanks,' I managed to say. I don't know how.

We sat in silence after she'd gone.

'It's me, isn't it,' I said eventually, staring ahead of me at nothing.

'Do you want it to be?'

'I don't know *what* I want. I don't even know who I *am* any more.'

Shona swam in front of me and made me look at her. 'Emily, maybe we can find out more. He's still alive! He's out there somewhere!'

'Yeah, in prison. For life.'

'But at least he didn't want to leave you!'

Perhaps he still thought about me. Perhaps I *could* find out more.

'I think we should go back to the shipwreck,' Shona said.

'*What?* No way!'

'Think about it! Your mum's dream, what Mrs Tailspin said in the lesson. They might have gone there together!'

Maybe she was right. I didn't have any better ideas. 'I'll think about it,' I said. 'Give me a few days.'

'Wednesday, then.'

'OK.'

'Look, I'd better be heading back.' I slithered over to the spirally tube.

'Will you be all right?'

'Yeah.' I tried to smile. Would I? That was anyone's guess.

I swam home through the silent water, my thoughts as crowded and unfathomable as the sea.

Chapter Seven

'*A*re you eating that or playing with it?' Mum asked over the top of her glasses as I stirred my cereal, watching the milk turn brown and the flakes fade into a soggy beige.

'What? Huh? Oh, sorry.' I took a mouthful, then stirred some more.

Mum had the *Observer* spread out in front of her. She flicked through the pages, tutting every now and then, or frowning and pushing her glasses further up her nose.

How was I ever going to find out what was going on? It's not exactly the kind of thing that crops up over your Sunday breakfast: 'Oh, by the way, Mum, I've been meaning to ask. I don't suppose you married a merman, had his child and then never saw

77

him again? OR THOUGHT TO TELL YOUR DAUGHTER ABOUT IT? *HUH???*'

I squelched my cereal against the side of the bowl, splashing milk onto the table.

'Careful, love.' Mum wiped the edge of her paper with her hand. Then she looked at me. 'Are you all right? It's not like you not to eat your breakfast.'

'I'm fine.' I got up and emptied my bowl into the sink.

'Emily?'

I ignored her as I sat back down at the table and pulled at my hair, winding it round in my fingers.

Mum took her glasses off. That meant it was serious. Then she folded her arms. Double serious. 'I'm waiting,' she said, her mouth tight, her eyes small. '*Emily*, I said I'm —'

'Why do you never talk about my dad?'

Mum jerked in her seat as though I'd punched her. '*What?*'

'You never talk about my father,' I said, my voice coming out quieter this time. 'I don't know anything about him. It's as though he never existed.'

Mum put her glasses back on; then she took them off again and got up. She lit a gas ring, put the kettle on it and gazed at the flickering flame. 'I don't know what to *say*,' she muttered eventually.

'Why not start by telling me something about him?'

'I want to. Darling, of course I want to.'

'So how come you never have done?'

Her eyes had gone all watery and she rubbed them with the sleeve of her cardigan. 'I don't know. I just can't – I can't do it.'

If there's one thing I can't *bear*, it's Mum crying. 'Look, it's OK. I'm sorry.' I got out of my seat and put my arms round her shoulders. 'It doesn't matter.'

'But it *does*.' She wiped her nose with the edge of the tablecloth. 'I want to tell you. But I can't, I can't, I – '

'It's OK, Mum, honest. You don't have to tell me.'

'But I want to,' she sobbed. 'I just can't remember!'

'You can't *remember*?' I let go and stared at her. 'You don't remember the man you married?'

She looked at me through bloodshot eyes. 'Well, yes – no. I mean, sometimes I think I remember things. But then it goes again. Disappears.'

'Disappears.'

'Just like he did,' she said quietly, her body shaking, her head in her hands. 'I can't even remember my own husband. Your father. Oh, I'm a terrible mother.'

'Don't start that,' I sighed. 'You're a brilliant mother. The best.'

'Really?' She smoothed down her skirt against her lap. I forced myself to smile. She looked up and stroked my cheek with her thumb. 'I must have done something right to get you, eh?' she said weakly.

I stood up. 'Look. Just forget it. It doesn't matter. OK?'

'You deserve better than –'

'Come on, Mum. It's all right,' I said firmly. 'Hey, how about some pocket money?'

She pinched my cheek. 'Munchkin,' she sniffed. 'Pass me my purse then.'

She handed me two pound coins and I headed down the pier.

I dawdled as I made my way past the amusement arcade. Not fair. Nothing was fair. I couldn't even have a go on the penny roll. I didn't need Mandy turning up and having a go at me on top of everything else.

I bought some candyfloss from the end of the pier and wandered down to the prom, my head filled with thoughts and questions. I didn't notice Mr Beeston coming towards me.

'Watch yourself,' he said as I nearly walked into him.

'Sorry. Miles away.'

He smiled at me in that way that always gives me weird shivers in my neck and arms. One side of his mouth turned up, the other reaching down and his crooked teeth poking out through the dark gap in between.

'How's Mum?' he asked.

That's when I had a thought. Mr Beeston had been around a long time. He was kind of friendly with

Mum. Maybe he'd know something.

'She's not all that great, actually,' I said as I bit into the top of my candyfloss, warm fluff melting into sugar in my mouth.

'Oh? Why so?'

'She's a bit sad about . . . some things.'

'Things? What "*things*"?' he said quickly, his smile gone.

'Just . . .'

'Is she ill? What's the matter?' Mr Beeston's face turned hard as he narrowed his eyes at me.

'Well, my father . . .' I pulled at my candyfloss and a long piece came away like a loose thread from a fluffy pink jumper. I folded it over into my mouth.

'Your *what*?' Mr Beeston burst out. What *was* his problem?

'I was asking her about my father and she got upset.'

He lowered his voice. 'What did she tell you?'

'That's just it, you see. She didn't tell me anything.'

'Nothing at all?'

'She said she couldn't remember anything. Then she started crying.'

'Couldn't remember anything? That's what she said?'

I nodded.

'You're quite sure now? Nothing at all?'

'Yes. Nothing.'

'Right then.' Mr Beeston breathed out hard through his nose. It made a low whistling sound.

81

'So, I wondered if you could help me.'

'Me? How on earth can *I* help you?' he snapped.

'I just wondered if she'd ever talked to you about him. With you being her friend and everything.'

He examined my face, squeezing his eyes down to narrow slits as he stared. I wanted to run away. Of course he wouldn't know anything. Why would she talk to him and not me? I tried to hold his eyes but he was staring at me so hard I had to look away.

He took hold of me by my elbow and pointed up the promenade with his other hand. 'I think it's time you and I had a little chat,' he said.

I tried to shake my elbow away as we walked but he held it tighter and paced faster. We'd got all the way to the end of the promenade before he let go and motioned for me to sit down on a bench.

'Now listen to me and listen well because I'll tell you this once and once only.'

I waited.

'And I don't want you bothering your mother with it. You've upset her enough already.'

'But I –'

'Never mind, never mind,' he raised his hand to stop me. 'You weren't to know.'

He wiped his forehead with a hanky. 'Now then,' he said, shifting his weight onto his side as he put his hanky away. His trousers had a hole just below the pocket. 'Your father and I, we used to be friends. Best friends. Even thought we were brothers, some folk did; that's how close we were.'

Brothers? Surely Mr Beeston was loads older than my father? I opened my mouth to speak.

'Like my kid brother he was. Did everything together.'

'Like what?'

'What?'

'What things did you do? I want to know what he was like.'

'All the things young lads get up to,' he snapped. 'We went fishing together. Went out on our bikes – '

'Motorbikes?'

'Yes, yes, motorbikes, pushbikes – the lot. Did it together. Best friends, we were. Chased the girls together, too.'

Mr Beeston chasing girls. I shuddered.

He cleared his throat. 'Then of course, he met your mother and things changed.'

'Changed? How?'

'Well, one might say they fell in love. At least, she did. Very much so.'

'And what about my dad?'

'He did a very good impression of love. For a while. He certainly didn't want to fool around with cars any more.'

'I thought it was bikes.'

'Cars, bikes – whatever. He wasn't interested. Spent all their time together.'

Mr Beeston stared into the distance, his hands in his pockets. He looked as though he was struggling with something. Then he jingled his coins and said, 'But of course it didn't last. Your father turned out not to be the gentleman he'd had us believe he was.'

'What do you mean?'

'This is a rather delicate matter. But I shall tell you. Let us say he wasn't the most *responsible* person. He was happy enough to lead your mother up the garden path, but not prepared to stay by her side when they got to the gate.'

'Huh?'

His face reddened. 'He was content to sow but not reap.'

'Mr Beeston, I don't know what you're going on about.'

'Good grief, child. I'm talking about responsibility,' he snapped. 'Where do you think *you* came from?'

'D'you mean he got my mum pregnant with me and then ran off?'

'Yes, yes, that is what I mean.'

Why didn't you say so then? I wanted to say – but didn't dare. Mr Beeston looked so angry. 'So he left her?' I asked, just to make sure I'd got it right.

'Yes, he left her,' he replied through tight lips.

'Where did he go?'

'That's just it. No one ever heard from him again.

84

The strain was obviously too much for him,' he said sarcastically.

'What strain?'

'Fatherhood. Good for nothing layabout, he was. Never willing to grow up and take responsibility.' Mr Beeston looked away. 'What he did – it was despicable,' he said, his voice becoming raspy. 'I shall never forgive him.' He got up from the bench, his face hard and set. 'Never,' he repeated. Something about the way he said it made me hope I'd never get on his wrong side.

I followed him as we carried on along the prom. 'Didn't anyone try to find him?'

'Find him?' Mr Beeston looked at me, but it was as though he was seeing through me. His eyes wouldn't meet mine. 'Find him?' he repeated. 'Yes – of course we tried. No one could have done more than I did. Travelled the country for weeks, put up posters. We even had a message on the radio, begging him to come home and meet his – well, his . . .'

'His daughter?'

Mr Beeston didn't reply.

'So he never even saw me?'

'We did everything we could.'

I looked down the promenade, trying to take in what I'd heard. It *couldn't* be true. Could it? A young couple ambled towards us, the man holding a baby up in the air, the woman laughing, a spaniel jumping up between them. Further down, an elderly couple were walking slowly against the wind, arms linked.

'I think I need to go now,' I said. We'd walked all the way round to the lighthouse.

Mr Beeston pulled me back by my arm. 'You're not to talk to your mother about this, do you hear me?'

'Why not?'

'You saw what happened. It's far too painful for her.' He tightened his grip, his fingers biting into my arm. 'Promise me you won't mention it.'

I didn't say anything.

Mr Beeston looked hard into my eyes. 'People can block things out completely if the memory is too much to cope with. That's a scientific fact. There'll be all sorts of trouble if you try and make her talk about this.' He pulled on my arm, his face inches from mine. 'And you don't want trouble – do you?' he said in a whisper.

I shook my head.

'*Do* you?' he repeated with another yank on my arm.

'No – of course not,' my voice wobbled.

He smiled his wonky smile at me and let go of my arm. 'Good,' he said. 'Good. Now, am I seeing you this afternoon?'

'I'm going out,' I said quickly. I'd think of something to do. I couldn't cope with Sunday tea with Mum and Mr Beeston. Especially now.

'Very well. Tell your mother I'll be round at three o'clock.'

'Yeah.'

We stood by the lighthouse. For a moment, I had a vision of him throwing me inside and locking me in! Why would he do that? He'd never done anything to hurt me – before today. I rubbed my arm. I could still feel the pinch of his fingers digging into my skin. But it was nothing compared with the disappointment I felt in my chest. Jake *wasn't* my father, after all, if Mr Beeston was to be believed. And he had no reason to lie – did he? Nothing made sense any more.

'Now, let's see, where's the, hm . . .' Mr Beeston talked to himself as he fumbled with his keys. He had about five keyrings rattling on a long chain. But then he gasped. 'What the – where's my . . .'

'What's wrong?'

He ignored me. 'It can't be missing. It can't be.' He felt in his trouser pockets, pulling the insides out and shaking his hanky. 'It was here. I'm sure it was.'

'The lighthouse key?'

'No, not the lighthouse key, the – ' He stopped fumbling and looked up at me, as if he'd only just remembered I was there, his eyes dark and hard. 'You're still here,' he said. 'Go on. Leave me be. But don't forget our chat. It's between you and me. Remember, you don't want to cause any *trouble*.' Then he unlocked the lighthouse door. 'I've got some important things to do,' he said. Squinting into my eyes, he added, 'I'll see you again soon.' For some reason, it sounded like a threat.

Before I had a chance to say anything else, he'd slipped inside and shut the door behind him. A second later, a bolt slid across.

As I turned to leave, I kicked something up in the dust. It glinted at me. A keyring. I picked it up. A brass plate with crystals round the edges. There was a picture engraved on one side. A pitchfork or something.

Two keys hung from the ring: one big chunky one, the other a little metal one the same as Mum has for our suitcase. A tiny gold chain hung from the plate, a clasp at its other end open and broken.

I banged on the lighthouse door and waited. 'Mr Beeston!' I called. I banged once more.

Nothing.

I looked at the keyring again, running my fingers over its crystal edge. Oh well. I could always give it back another time.

I buttoned the keyring into my pocket and headed home.

Chapter Eight

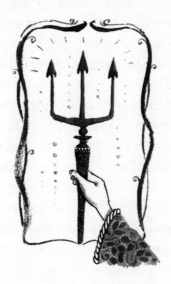

*T*his was it. The moment I'd been dreading. I stepped through the trough of icy cold water on the way to the pool. I'd tried telling Mr Bird I had a verruca but he just gave me a couple of white rubber socks to put on my feet. So now the game was up *and* I looked ridiculous. Great. What was I going to *do*? Five more minutes and my secret would be revealed. Everyone would know I was a *freak*!

'Come on people; we haven't got all day.' Bob clapped his hands together as I walked slowly to the side of the pool and joined the rest of the class. 'It'll be time to get out again before you set foot in the water.'

My heart thumped so loud I could feel it in my ears.

'Right, those who can swim can get on with it,' he said. *Please don't remember, please don't remember*, I prayed silently. Time was running out; I *had* to think of something.

'That means *you*.' Mandy Rushton elbowed Julie and pointed to me. 'What's up, *fish girl*?' she sneered. 'Gone shy all of a sudden?'

I tried to ignore her but Bob was looking our way. 'What's going on over –' Then he spotted me. 'Ah yes. One that got cramp, isn't it?'

I stepped back towards the wall, hoping it might swallow me up and I'd disappear forever. I couldn't do it – I *couldn't!*

'You can get in when you're ready.' *Yeah, right – no way.* 'Take it easy, though. Don't want the same thing to happen.' He turned back to the others. 'Right, you guys. Let's get on with it, shall we?'

'Go on then – let's all see how the *fish girl* does it!' Mandy said loudly and everyone around us turned to look. Then she pushed me forward and I lost my footing. Tripping on the slippy floor, I went flying into the pool with a loud SPLASH!

For the tiniest moment, I forgot all about Mandy. She wasn't important. All that mattered was that I was in the water again, losing myself to its creamy smoothness, wrapping myself up in it as if it was my favourite dressing-gown, keeping me safe and warm.

Then I remembered where I was!

I swam to the surface and looked up to see thirty pairs of eyes facing my way – at least one of them glinting nastily at me, waiting for my FREAKNESS to be revealed!

I had to fight it – I had to! But it was starting already! My legs were going numb, joining together. And, like an idiot, I'd swum halfway across the pool!

I heaved myself through the water, splashing and dragging my body along, keeping my legs as still as possible to try and stop my tail from forming. Bit by bit, I propelled myself to the side, my arms working like a windmill. I *had* to get there before it happened. Hurry, hurry!

Gasping and panting, I finally heaved myself out of the pool – JUST in time! The second I dragged my body over the side, my legs started to relax. Wheezing and breathless, I pulled myself out of the pool and sat on the side.

Bob was over in a second. 'Have you hurt yourself?' He stared down at me and I suddenly had an idea. I grabbed my foot.

'It's my ankle,' I said. 'I think I've sprained it.'

Bob narrowed his eyes. 'How did this happen?'

I was about to say I'd fallen in when I saw Mandy's face. Sneering and jeering at me. Why should I let her off? 'Mandy pushed me,' I said.

'Right, well there'll be no swimming for either of you this week,' he said. 'You can sit in the corner for the rest of the lesson,' he said crossly to Mandy. Then he turned to me. 'And you'd better get that ankle rested.'

He clapped his hands as he went back to the class. 'Right, people, show's over. Let's do some swimming, shall we?'

It wasn't the cold that made me shiver as I limped back to the changing room. It was more to do with Mandy's words, hissed at me through clenched teeth so quietly no one else could hear.

'I'll get you back for this, fish girl,' she said. 'Just you wait.'

I hung back while Shona swam ahead, my tail flapping as we drew nearer to the shipwreck. The night was crunchy with a million stars. No moon.

'Nearly there.' Shona dived under the water. I followed her, trailing a few metres behind.

Soon, the golden light was filtering through weeds and rocks, pulling us towards the ship.

'Shona, we can't do it!' I blurted out. 'There's no point.'

Shona swam back to me. 'But you agreed – '

'It's no good. He's not my father.'

She stared at me.

'My father left us. Just like I thought he had.' I told

her what Mr Beeston had said – and about his strange veiled threat.

'Are you sure?' she asked when I'd finished.

Why would he lie? I'd asked myself that question so many times over the last three days. I still wasn't sure I believed him – but it was better than building up false hopes.

'I was so certain . . .' Shona looked over her shoulder at the ship. 'Look – why don't we go anyway? We're nearly there.'

'What's the use?'

'What have we got to lose? And there was something I wanted to show you. Something about the door in that passageway.'

What did it matter? The ship didn't have anything to do with me. There was nothing to fear. 'OK,' I said.

We slithered down the dark corridor, feeling our way back down those slimy walls. I tried hard not to make eye contact with the open-jawed fish that had followed us down.

'So what did you want to show me?' I asked as we swam.

'There was a symbol on the door. I completely forgot about it after everything that happened.'

'What symbol?'

'A trident.'

'What's one of those?'

'Neptune's symbol. He carries it everywhere with him. It's what he uses to create thunderstorms – or islands.'

'*Islands?* He can create whole islands?'

'Well, that's only when he's in a good mood – so it doesn't happen much. More often he makes the *biggest* storms out at sea!' Shona's eyes had that wide shiny look they always did when she talked about Neptune.

'Some merfolk say he can turn you to stone with his trident. His palace is filled with stone animals. I heard that they were all animals who had disobeyed him at one time. And he can make ships disappear, just by waving it at them – or produce a feast for a hundred merpeople, or create volcanoes out of thin air.'

'Cool!'

We'd arrived at the door. 'Look.' She pointed at the top corner of the door. A brass plate. An engraving. Quite faint – but there was no mistaking what I was looking at.

The picture from Mr Beeston's keyring.

'But – but that's – ' I pulled at my pocket. 'It's impossible. It *can't* be!'

'What?' Shona swam up to my side. I handed her the keyring. 'Where did you get this?' she asked.

'It's Mr Beeston's.' But it *couldn't* be! I'd made a mistake. I must have done!

'Sharks!' Shona breathed. 'So d'you think . . .' Her

words trailed away into the watery darkness. What *did* I think? I didn't think anything any more.

'Shall we try it?' Shona took the key from me.

I watched in amazement as it turned smoothly in the lock.

The door slid open.

Silently, we slithered inside. We were in a small office. It had a desk stacked about a metre high with laminated folders and papers held down by rocks, and a stool nailed to the floor in front of it. Shona swam to the desk and pulled on something. A second later, an orange glow burst out above me. I blinked as I got used to the sudden glare, then looked up to see where the light had come from. A long slimy creature with a piece of string on its tail clung to the ceiling.

'Electric eel,' she explained.

We looked at each other in silence. 'What about the other key?' she said eventually, swimming over to a metal filing cabinet in the corner. I tried the drawers but they wouldn't pull out. I almost closed my eyes as I tried to put it in the lock at the top. *Please don't fit, please don't fit*, I said to myself. What would I find if it did?

I couldn't even get it halfway in.

I let out a huge breath and was suddenly desperate to get out of there. 'Shona, maybe this is all a big mistake,' I said, backing out of the office. But then I knocked my tail against the stool and slipped backwards. A swarm of tiny black fish escaped from under the table, spinning out of the room and away from us.

'Emily!' Shona tugged my sleeve and pointed at something under the table.

I leaned forward to get a closer look. A wooden chest. Quite big, with brass edging and a chain looped all around it. It was like something out of *Treasure Island*. I swam under the table and Shona helped me drag it out. 'Flipping fins,' she said quietly, staring at something dangling at the front of the chain. A brass padlock.

As I slipped the key easily into the lock and the brass hook bounced open, I wasn't even surprised. A line of silver fish pecked at the chest as I opened it. It was full of files. I grabbed a handful of them. The colours changed from blue to green as I lifted them towards me. Rummaging through the pile, I pulled the rest of them out. Then I came to a folder that was different from the rest. For one thing, it was thicker than the others. For another thing, it looked newer.

And for another, it had my name on it.

Chapter Nine

J don't know how long I looked at the file. I realised at some point that my hand had almost gone numb from clutching it so tightly.

'What is it?' Shona came to look over my shoulder at the files. That's when I noticed another one at the bottom of the chest. I reached down to get it. It had my mum's name on it. Below that was another. I almost didn't dare to look at that one. I shut my eyes as I picked it up. When I opened them, I was looking at a name I'd been dreaming about for a week: Jake Windsnap.

I traced the words with my fingertips. Jake Windsnap. I said his name over and over, wondering if there was any way it could be a mistake or a practical joke or something. 'Jake *is* my father,' I said out loud.

Of *course* he was. I'd known it in my heart from the first time I'd heard his name. It just took seeing it in writing to convince my brain.

I opened the file, my hands shaking so much I almost dropped all its contents. The sheets inside it were plastic. And they all had the pitchfork image at the top: Neptune's trident.

'But what in sharks' name does Mr Beeston have to do with any of this?' Shona asked.

'Maybe he knows where my dad is, after all. I mean, if they were best friends, maybe he's trying to help him. Maybe they've been in touch all along.' My words came out in a rush, none of them convincing me – or Shona, by the look on her face.

'There's only one way to find out,' she said.

I held the files out in front of me. Once I'd looked inside, there would be no going back. I couldn't pretend I hadn't seen whatever was in there. Maybe I didn't want to know. I pulled at my hair, twiddling, twisting it round and round. I *had* to look. Whatever it said, I needed to know the truth.

I opened the file with my name on it. A scrappy bit of paper with a handwritten note scrawled across it fell on the floor. I picked it up, Shona looking over my shoulder as I read.

EW One: All clear.
   Nothing to report. No mer-gene identified. Possibly negative. (50% chance.) Scale detection nil.

'What in the ocean is that meant to mean?'

I shook my head, pulling a bigger sheet out of the file.

> *EW Eight: Moment of truth?*
> *Subject has requested swimming lessons again. (See MPW file for cross-ref.) CFB present to witness request. Denied by mother. Unlikely to be granted in near future. Needs careful attention. Almost certainly negative mer-gene but experiment MUST NOT be abandoned. Continued observation – priority.*

'Subject!' I spluttered. 'Is that me?'

Shona winced.

Careful watch? Had he been stalking me? What if he was watching us now? I shuddered and swam over to close the office door. A lone blue fish skimmed into the room and over my head as I did.

We scanned the rest of the file. It was all the same: subjects and initials and weird stuff that didn't make sense.

I picked up my mum's file.

> *MPW Zero: Objectives.*
> *MPW – greatest risk to mer-world detection. Constant supervision by CFB. M-Drug to be administered.*

Shona gasped. 'M-Drug. I know what that is! They're wiping her memory!'

'*What*? Who is?'

'Mr Beeston. He must work for Neptune!'

'Work for Neptune? But how? I mean, he *can't* do. Can he?'

Shona rubbed her lip. 'They usually send them away afterwards, though.'

'Why?'

'It can wear off if you go near merfolk areas. We did all about it in science last term.'

'So you think they did it to my mum?'

'They probably still are. One dose is usually enough for a one-off incident – but not for a whole series of memories. They must be topping it up somehow.'

Topping it up? I thought about all Mr Beeston's visits. He wasn't lonely after all! He was drugging my mum!

We looked all the way through Mum's file. Page after page noting her movements. He'd been spying on us for *years*.

'I feel sick,' I said, closing the file.

Shona picked up Jake's file. There was a note stuck on the front with something scribbled on it. *East Wing: E 930.* We read in silence.

JW Three: Bad influence.

JW continuing to complain about sentence. Sullen and difficult.

JW Eight: Improvement

Subject has settled into routine of prison life. Behaviour improved.

JW Eleven: Isolation
Operation Desert Island discussed openly by prisoner.
Isolation – three days.

'Operation Desert Island!' Shona breathed. 'So it's true after all. There *is* a place! Somewhere merfolk and humans live together!'

'How d'you know that's what it is?' I asked. 'It could be anything.'

We read on.

'None of it makes any sense,' I said, swimming backwards and forwards across the room to help me think.

Shona carried on flicking through the file. 'It's all numbers and dates and weird initials.' She closed the file. 'I can't make fin or tail of it.' She grabbed another file from the chest. 'Listen to this,' she said. '"Project Lighthouse. CFB to take over Brightport Lighthouse until completion of Windsnap problem. Ground floor adapted for access. Occasional siren support available with 'unreliable' beam. Previous lighthouse keeper: M-drug and removal from scene."' Shona looked up.

'What are we going to do?' I whispered.

'What *can* we do? But hey – at least you've found your dad.'

My dad. The words sounded strange. Not right. Not yet. 'But I *haven't* found him,' I said. 'That's just it. All I've found is some stupid file that doesn't make any sense.'

Shona put the file down. 'I'm sorry.'

'Look, Shona, we know Jake's my – my father, don't we?'

'Without a doubt.'

'And we know where he is?'

'Well, yes.'

'And he can't come out. He's locked away. And he didn't *choose* to leave me . . .'

'I'm *sure* he never wanted to –'

'So we'll go to him!'

Shona looked at me blankly.

I shoved the files back in the chest, locked it firmly. 'Come on, let's go!'

'Go? Where?'

'The prison.' I turned round to face her. 'I've got to find him.'

Shona's tail flapped gently. 'Emily. It's *miles* away.'

'We're mermaids! We can swim for miles, no problem!'

'Maybe *I* can, but it's definitely too far for you. You're only half mermaid, remember.'

'So you're saying I'm not as good as you?' I folded my arms. 'I thought you were meant to be my friend. I even thought you might have been my best friend.'

Shona's tail flapped even more. 'Really?' she said. 'I want you to be my best friend, too.'

'Well, you've got a funny way of showing it. You won't even help me find my father.'

Shona winced. 'I just don't think we'd make it there. I'm not even sure exactly where it *is*.'

'But we'll never know if we don't try. Please, Shona. If you were *really* my best friend, you would.'

'OK,' she sighed. 'We'll try. But I don't want you collapsing on me miles out at sea. If you get tired, you have to tell me, and we come back, OK?'

I shoved the chest back under the table. 'OK.'

I don't know how long we'd been swimming. Maybe an hour. I started to feel as if I had heavy weights attached to each arm; my tail was practically dropping off. Flying fish raced along with us, bouncing past on both sides. An occasional gull darted into the sea, a white dart piercing the water.

'How much further is it?' I gasped.

'We're not even halfway yet.' Shona looked back. 'Are you all right?'

'Fine.' I tried not to pant while I spoke. 'Great. No problem.'

Shona slowed down to swim alongside me and we carried on in silence for a bit. 'You're not OK, are you?' she said after a while.

'I'm fine,' I repeated but my head slipped under the water while I spoke. I coughed as a mouthful of water went down the wrong way. Shona grabbed me.

'Thanks.' I wriggled away from her. 'I'm all right now.'

She looked at me doubtfully. 'Maybe we could

both do with a rest,' she said. 'There's a tiny island about five minutes' swim from here. It's out of our way, but it would give us a chance to get our breath back.'

'OK,' I said. 'If you really need to, I don't mind.'

'Great.' Shona swam off again. 'Follow me.'

Soon, we were sitting on an island barely larger than the flat rock that had become our meeting place. It was hard and gravelly but I lay down the second I dragged myself out of the sea, the water brushing against me as my tail turned back into legs.

It seemed only seconds later that Shona gently shook my shoulder. 'Emily,' she whispered. 'You'd better get up. It's starting to get light.'

I sat up. 'How long have I been asleep?'

Shona shrugged. 'Not long.'

'Why didn't you wake me? We'll never get there now. You did it on purpose!'

Shona squeezed her lips together and scrunched up her eyes. I thought about her pretending she needed a rest, and about taking me to her school and everything. 'I'm sorry,' I said. 'I know you didn't do it on purpose.'

'It's too far. It's probably even too far for me, never mind you.'

'I'm *never* going to see him. I bet he doesn't even remember he's got a daughter!' I felt a drop of salty water on my cheek and wiped it roughly away. 'What am I going to do?'

Shona put her arm round me. 'I'm sorry,' she said.

'I'm sorry, too. I shouldn't have been mean to you. You've been brilliant. Really helpful.'

Shona pulled a face at me, as if she was trying not to smile but couldn't stop a little grin from slipping out through her frown.

'And I know you're right,' I added. 'There's no way I could get there tonight, not if we're only half way.'

'Not even that. Look.' She pointed out to the horizon. 'See that big cloud that looks like a whale spurting water – with the little starfish-shaped one behind it?'

I looked up at the sky. 'Um, yeah,' I said uncertainly.

'Just below that, where the sea meets the sky, it's lighter than the rest of the horizon.'

I studied the horizon. It looked an awfully long way away!

'That's it. The Great Mermer Reef. It's like a huge wall, bigger than anything you've ever seen in your life, made of rocks and coral in every shape and colour you could imagine – and then about a hundred more. The prison's a mile beyond it. You have to go through the reef to get there.'

My heart felt like a rock itself – dropping down to the bottom of the sea. 'Shona, it's absolutely *miles* away.'

'We'll work something out,' Shona said. 'I promise.' Then she scrabbled around among the rocks and picked up a couple of stones. She handed one to me.

'What's this?' I looked at the stone.

'They're friendship pebbles. They mean that we're best friends – if you want to be.'

'Of course I want to be!'

'Look, they're almost exactly the same.' She showed me her pebble. 'We each keep them on us at all times. It means we'll always be there for each other.' Then she said, more quietly, 'And it's also a promise that we'll find your dad.'

I washed my pebble in the water; it went all shiny and smooth. 'It's the best present anyone's ever given me.'

Shona slipped hers into her tail and I put mine in my jacket pocket. I didn't want it to disappear when my legs returned! I looked at the patch of light spreading and growing across the horizon.

'Come on.' Shona slid back into the sea. 'We'd better get going.'

We slowly made our way back to Rainbow Rocks.

'See you Sunday?' I asked as we said goodbye.

Shona's cheeks reddened a touch. 'Can we make it Monday?'

'I thought you couldn't get out on Mondays.'

'I will. I'll make sure of it. Just that it's the Diving and Dance display Monday morning and I don't want to be too tired for the triple flips.'

'Monday then.' I smiled. 'And good luck.'

By the time I got home, I was so tired I could have fallen asleep standing up. But my head was spinning with thoughts and questions. And sadness. I'd found out where my father was, but how would we ever get there? Would we really find him? It felt like I was losing him all over again. I'd virtually lost my mum as well. If only I could make her remember!

As I tried to get to sleep, something Shona had said swam into the corner of my mind. *Sometimes it doesn't work at all, especially if you go near merfolk areas.*

Of course!

I knew *exactly* what I was going to do.

Chapter Ten

*M*um always sleeps in on Sundays. She says even God had a day of rest and she doesn't see why she can't. I'm not allowed to disturb her until she says it's morning – which isn't usually till about midday.

I paced up and down the boat, willing her to wake up. What if she slept right through till the afternoon? Disaster! I couldn't take the risk of Mr Beeston turning up before I'd spoken to her. So I broke a Golden Rule. I crept into her room and sat on the bed.

'Mum,' I stage-whispered from the end of the bed. She didn't stir. I inched further up and leaned towards her ear. 'Mum,' I croaked a bit louder.

She opened one eye and then closed it again. 'Whadyouwan?' she grumbled.

'You have to get up.'

'Whassamatter?'

'I want to go out.'

Mum groaned and turned over.

'Mum, I want us to go out together.'

Silence.

'Please get up.'

She turned back to face me and opened her eyes a crack.

'We never do anything together,' I said.

'Why now? Why can't you leave me in peace? What time is it, anyway?'

I quickly turned her alarm clock round so she couldn't see it. 'It's late. Come on, Mum. *Please*.'

Mum rubbed her eyes and lay on her back. 'I don't suppose you're going to give me any peace until I do, are you?'

I smiled hopefully.

'Just leave me alone and I'll get up.'

I didn't move. 'How do I know you won't go back to sleep the minute I leave?'

'Emily! I said I'll get up and I will. Now leave me alone! And if you want to get back in my good books, you can make me a nice cup of tea. And then I might just forgive you.'

Mum took a bite of her toast. 'So, where do you fancy going, now you've ruined my Sunday morning for me?'

I knew *exactly* where we were going. Shiprock Bay. The nearest you could get to Rainbow Rocks by road. I'd been studying the bus routes and there was one that took us virtually all the way there. We could get off on the coast road and walk along the headland. It must be worth a go. I had to jog her memory somehow.

'I just thought we could have a day trip round the coast,' I said casually as I popped a piece of toast and marmalade in my mouth.

'What about Mr Beeston?'

'What about him?' I nearly choked on my marmalade.

'We'll have to be back for three. Can't let him down.'

'Oh, Mum! Can't you break your date with him for once?'

'Emily. Mr Beeston is a lonely man and a good friend. How many times do I have to tell you that? You know I don't like to let him down. He has not broken our arrangement once in all these years, and I'm not about to do the same. And it is *not* a date!'

'Whatever.' This wasn't the time to tell her what I knew about the 'lonely man'. What *did* I know, anyway? Nothing that made any sense. I swallowed hard to get my toast down. My throat was dry. We'd still have time to get there. Maybe we could accidentally-on-purpose miss the bus back. I'd think of something. I *had* to!

'This is quite nice, actually.' Mum looked out of the window as we bumped round the coast road. It had started to turn inland and I was trying to work out the best stop to get off. The sea looked *completely* different from this angle. Then I saw a familiar clump of rocks and decided to take a chance. I got up and rang the bell. 'This is our stop,' I said.

'You know, I think I'm almost glad you got me up,' Mum said as we got off the bus. 'Not that that's an excuse to do it every week!' She walked over to a green bench on the headland that looked out to sea and sat down. 'And you've picked such a nice spot, too.'

'What are you doing?' I asked as she reached into her bag and brought out the sandwiches.

'We're having a picnic, aren't we?'

'Not *here*!'

Mum looked round. 'I can't see anywhere better.'

'Mum, we're right by the road! Let's walk out towards the sea a bit.'

She frowned.

'Come on, just a little way. *Please*. You promised.'

'I did no such thing!' she snapped. But she put the sandwiches back anyway and we headed along a little headland path that led out towards the sea.

After we'd been walking for about fifteen minutes,

the path came to an abrupt end. In front of us was a gravelly climb down the cliff.

'Now what?' Mum looked round.

'Let's go down there.'

'You must be joking. Have you seen my shoes?'

I looked at her feet. Why hadn't I thought to tell her not to wear her platform sandals? 'They're OK,' I said.

'Emily. I am *not* going to break my ankles just so you can drag me off down some dangerous cliffs.' She turned round and started walking back.

'No, wait!' I looked around desperately. She mustn't leave – she had to see the rocks. A winding path lay almost hidden under brambles. Stony and rough but not as steep as the other one. 'Let's try here,' I said. 'And look – it goes flat again over there if we can just get down this bit.'

'I don't know.' Mum looked doubtfully down the cliff.

'Come on; let's try it. I'll go first and then I can cushion your fall if you go flying.' I tried a cheeky smile, and she gave in.

'If I break my legs, it's breakfast in bed every day until I'm better.'

'Deal.'

I picked my way through the brambles and stones, checking behind me every few seconds to make sure Mum was still there. We managed to get to the rocks in one piece.

Mum rubbed her elbow. 'Ouch. Nettles.' She

pulled at a dock leaf and rubbed it on her arm. I gazed in front of us. A few metres of sea separated us from Rainbow Rocks. I couldn't help smiling as I watched the sea washing over the flat rocks, rainbow water caressing them with every wave.

'Mum?'

'Hm?'

I took a deep breath. 'Do you believe in mermaids?' I asked, my throat tight and strained.

Mum laughed. 'Mermaids? Oh Emily, you don't half ask some silly –'

But then she stopped. She dropped the dock leaf on the ground. Looking out to sea, her face went all hard.

'What is it, Mum?' I asked gently.

'Where are we?' she whispered.

'Just by the coast. I just thought it'd be nice to go out for –'

'*What is this place?*'

I hadn't actually thought about what I'd say once we got here! What would she do if she knew – not just about Jake but about me, too? What if she only half remembered? She might think we were *both* freaks. Maybe she'd be ashamed of us. Why hadn't I thought this through?

I cleared my throat. 'Um. It's just some rocks,' I said carefully. 'Isn't it?'

Mum turned to me. 'I've been here before,' she said, her face scrunched up as if she was in pain.

'When?'

'I don't know. But I know this place.'

'Shall we go further down?'

'No!' She turned back the way we'd come. 'Emily. We have to go back. Mr Beeston will be expecting us.'

'But we've only just got here. Mr Beeston won't be round for ages yet.'

'I can't stay here,' Mum said. 'I've got a bad feeling about it. We're going home.' She started walking back so quickly I could hardly keep up.

We ate our sandwiches on that green bench on the headland, after all. A bus went whizzing past just as we were approaching the road so there was nothing for it but to wait. We ate in silence: me not knowing what to say, Mum gazing into space.

I kept wanting to ask her things, or tell her things, but where could I start?

Eventually another bus came and we rode home in silence as well. By the time we got back to Brightport pier, it was nearly four o' clock.

'Are you angry with me?' I asked as we let ourselves into the boat.

'Angry? Why? You haven't done anything wrong, have you?' Mum searched my face.

'I wanted to have a nice day out and now you've gone all sad.'

Mum shook her head. 'Just thoughtful, sweetheart. There was something about that place . . . ' Her voice trailed off.

'What? What was it?'

'It was such a strong memory, but I don't even know what it was.' She shook her head again and took her coat off. 'Listen to me, talking drivel as usual.'

'You're not talking drivel at all,' I said urgently. 'What was the memory?'

Mum hugged her coat. 'Do you know, it wasn't a memory of a *thing*. More a feeling of something. I felt an overwhelming feeling of . . . love.'

'Love?'

'And then something else. Sadness. Enormous sadness.' Mum took her coat down to the engine room to hang it up. 'I told you I was talking rubbish, didn't I?' she called. 'Now get that kettle on and I'll go and give Mr Beeston a shout. He'll be wondering where we got to.'

I glanced out of the window as I filled the kettle. Mr Beeston was on his way up the pier! My whole body shivered. He was pacing fast and didn't look happy.

POUND! POUND! POUND! He rapped on the roof as Mum came back in the kitchen.

'Oh good. He's here.' Mum went to let him in. 'Hello,' she smiled. 'I was just coming to – '

'Where have you been?' he demanded.

'We've been out for a day trip, haven't we Emily? Just along the –'

'Three o'clock I was here,' he snapped, stabbing a finger at his watch. 'An hour I waited. What's the meaning of this?' His head snapped across to face me. I swallowed hard.

Mum frowned at us both. 'Come on, no need to get upset,' she said. 'We'll have a nice cup of tea.' She went to get the cups and saucers. 'What have you got for us today, Mr B? Iced buns? Flapjacks?'

'Doughnuts,' he said without taking his eyes off me.

'I haven't done anything,' I said.

'Course you haven't, Emily. Now, are you joining us?' Mum held a cup out as Mr Beeston finally turned away. He took his jacket off and folded it over the back of a chair.

'No thanks.'

I lay on the sofa and eavesdropped, waiting for Mr Beeston to try to inject her with the memory drug. I had to catch him in the act, prove to Mum that he wasn't really her friend. But what if he got to me first? What if he injected *me* with the memory drug, too?

But he didn't do anything. As soon as he sat down with Mum, he acted as though nothing had happened. They just drank tea and munched doughnuts and chatted about B & B owners and the price of mini golf.

They'd hardly finished eating when Mr Beeston glanced at his watch. 'Well, that's me done,' he said.

'You're going?' But he hadn't drugged her yet!

Maybe he didn't do it every week. Well, I'd be waiting for him as soon as he tried!

'I have a 4.45 appointment,' he growled, the left side of his mouth twitching as he spoke. 'I don't like to keep people waiting.'

I didn't say anything.

'Goodbye, Mary P.' He let himself out.

Mum started clearing the cups away and I grabbed a tea towel.

'So, you were saying, earlier,' I began as Mum handed me a saucer.

'Saying?'

'About our outing.'

'Oh of course – the little trip to the headland,' Mum smiled. 'Lovely, wasn't it?'

'Not just the headland,' I said. 'The rocks.'

Mum looked at me blankly.

'Rainbow Rocks . . .' The words caught in my throat as I held my breath.

'Rainbow what?'

'Mum – don't tell me you've forgotten! The rocks, the rainbow colours when the sea washed over them, the way you felt when we were there. Love. And sadness and stuff?'

Mum laughed. 'You know, Mrs Partington told me you had a good imagination at the last parents' evening. Now I know what she means.'

I stared at her as she bustled about, straightening the tablecloth and brushing crumbs off the chairs with her hands.

'What?' She looked up.

'Mum, what do you think we were talking about before Mr Beeston came round?'

Mum shut one eye and rubbed her chin. 'Heck – give me a minute.' She looked worried for a moment, then laughed. 'You know – I can't remember. Gone! Never mind. Now fetch me the brush and pan. We're not leaving the carpet like this.'

I carried on staring at her. She'd forgotten! He *had* drugged her, after all! But how? And when?

'Come on, shape yourself. Brush and pan. Or do I have to get them myself?'

I fetched the brush and pan out of the cupboard and handed them to her.

'Mum . . . ' I tried again as she swept under the table. 'Do you *really* not remem–'

'*Emily*.' Mum sat up on her knees and spoke firmly. 'A joke is a joke, and it's usually not funny after a while. Now I don't want to hear any more rubbish about multicoloured rocks if you don't mind. I've got more important things to do than indulge your daydreams.'

'But it's not a –'

'EMILY.'

I knew that tone of voice. It meant it was time to shut up. I picked up the doughnut bags from the table and went to put them in the bin. Then I noticed some writing on one of the bags. *MPW*.

'Why has this one got your initials on?' I asked.

'I don't know. Probably so he knows which ones are mine.'

'What difference does it make?'

'Come on Emily, everyone knows I've got a sweet tooth. Mine had more sugar on.'

'But can't you tell which ones have more sugar just by looking at them?'

'*Emily*. Why are you being so *difficult* today? I *won't* have you talking about Mr Beeston like this. I'm not listening to another word.'

'But I don't understand! Why can't he just look in the bag?'

Mum ignored me. Then she started whistling and I gave up and went back to my cabin. I took the bags with me. They held some kind of answer, I was sure of it – if only I could work out what it was!

I stared so hard at her initials my eyes started to water.

And then, as the letters blurred under my gaze, it hit me so hard I nearly fell over. Of course! The memory drug!

It was in the doughnuts.

Chapter Eleven

*C*oming home from school on Monday, I slumped on the sofa and threw my bag on the floor. Mum was reading. 'Nice day?' she asked, folding over the corner of the page and putting her book down.

'Mm.' I got a glass of milk out of the fridge.

I could hardly bear to look at her. How was I ever going to get her to believe me? Somehow I had to make her see for herself what Mr Beeston was up to. *And* I still had to find Jake. What was I going to do?

A gentle rap on the roof startled me out of my thoughts. I clenched my fists. If that was Mr Beeston, I'd –

'Hello Emily,' Millie said in a mysterious kind of way as she unwrapped herself from her large black cloak.

'Are you going out?' I asked Mum.

'It's the Bay Residents' AGM. I told you last week.'

'Did you?'

'Nice to see I'm not the only one round here with the memory of a goldfish.' She tweaked my cheek as she passed me.

I checked my watch. 'But it's only six o'clock!'

'I need to get there early to open up. It's at the bookshop,' she called from down the corridor. 'Thanks for this, Millie,' she added as she came back in with her coat. 'Get the sofa bed out if I'm late.'

'I might just do that,' Millie replied. 'My energy is a little depleted today. I think it's the new Ginkgo Biloba tablets on top of my shiatsu.'

'Right,' Mum said, doing up her coat. Another knock on the roof made me jump again.

'Heck's becks Emily, you're a bit twitchy tonight, aren't you.' Mum ruffled my hair as Mr Beeston's face appeared at the door.

I froze.

'Only me,' he said, scanning the room without coming in.

'You didn't tell me *he* was going,' I whispered, grabbing at her coat as Mr Beeston waited outside.

'Of course he's going – he's the chairman!' she whispered back. 'And he's offered to help me set up,' she added. 'Which is nice of him, by the way.'

'Mum, I don't want you to go!'

'Don't want me to go? What on earth are you on about?'

What could I say? How could I get her to believe me? She wouldn't hear a word against Mr Beeston. The sweet, kind, lonely man. Well, I'd prove to her that he wasn't anything of the sort!

'I just –'

'Come on now. Don't be a baby.' She prised my fingers from her sleeve. 'Millie's here to look after you. I'm only up at the shop if you need me urgently. And I mean *urgently*.' She gave me a quick peck, rubbed my cheek with her thumb – and was gone.

'How come you don't go to the Bay Residents' meetings, Millie?'

'Oh I don't believe in all that democratic fuss and nonsense,' she said, shifting me up the sofa so she could sit down.

We sat silently in front of the telly. Once *Coronation Street* had finished, I waited for her to tell me it was bedtime. But she didn't. I looked across at the sofa; she lay on her side, her eyes closed, mouth slightly open.

'Millie?' I whispered. No reply. She was fast asleep!

Slinging my legs over the arm of my chair, I flicked channels. All boring. I settled on a programme about people doing mad stunts for no good reason. A woman who said she was scared of heights was about to do a bungee jump. *Why?*

I'd never seen anyone look so scared in my life. Her face was literally grey. As the camera zoomed out from her horrified eyes, she drew a breath – and then threw herself upside-down off the edge of the cliff!

After she'd done it, a little girl came running over to hug her. The woman was grinning like an idiot. 'I had to do it,' she said to the camera. 'Laura needs to go to America for an operation and I simply couldn't let her go alone, so I decided it was time to face my fears. Sometimes you just have to undo the ropes that bind you and go for it.' She hugged her daughter again; they were both crying. It was all a bit pukey, actually.

But later, as I brushed my teeth, the woman's words wouldn't leave me alone. There was something about them that seemed to be knocking on a door inside my mind. What was it? I ran them round and round in my head, until I was left with one phrase: 'Undo the ropes . . . and go for it.'

Oh crikey – that was it! That was what I had to do. The Great Mermer Reef might be too far to swim – but it wouldn't be too far by boat! And now was the perfect time. In fact, it might be my only chance.

Could I do it? *Really?* I looked at the bathroom clock. Half past eight. Mum wouldn't be back for ages yet and Millie was fast asleep in the other room. When would I get an opportunity like this again? I *had* to do it.

I grabbed the engine key and crept outside. There was probably another half an hour or so before it was dark. I could handle the darkness anyway; I'd got used to the sea at night.

But would I remember how to operate the boat? I'd only done it a few times. We have to go round to Southpool Harbour every couple of years to get the hull checked out and Mum usually lets me take it some of the way. We hardly ever use the sail. I don't know why we have it!

The promenade was quiet apart from the masts all clinking and chattering in the wind. I pulled at my hair, twisting it frantically round my fingers. I probably looked just like that woman before her bungee jump. But I knew how she felt, now. I simply *had* to do it, however dangerous or scary or mad it might be.

Pulling at the ropes, I had one last look down the pier. Deserted.

Almost.

Someone was coming out of the amusements. I ducked below the mast and waited. It was Mandy's mum! She was heading down the pier, probably to the meeting. A figure was standing in the doorway of the arcade. Mandy!

I ducked down again, waited for her to go back inside. Had she seen me?

The rope slackened in my hands – I was drifting away from the jetty. Close enough to jump back and pull the boat in again – but floating further away by the second. *What should I do?* There was still time to abandon the whole thing.

Then a breeze lifted the front of the boat off the

water and, without thinking, the decision was made. I glanced back at the amusements. She'd gone. I hurled the rope onto the jetty and turned the ignition key.

Nothing happened.

I tried again. It started this time, and I held my breath as its familiar 'dunka dunka' broke into the silence of the evening.

'OI!'

I turned to see who was shouting.

'Fish girl!'

Mandy! She stepped onto our jetty.

'What d'you think you're doing?' she called.

'Nothing!' *Nothing?* What kind of a stupid thing was that to say?

'Oh, I know. Are you running away, now Julie doesn't want to be your friend?'

'What?'

'She doesn't want to know you any more, after you dropped her last weekend. Good job she had me there to make her see *someone* cares about her feelings.' Mandy paused as she let an evil smile crawl across her face. 'Your mum knows you're taking the boat out, does she?'

'Course!' I said quickly. 'I'm just moving it round to Southpool.'

'Yeah, I'll bet. Shall we check, then?' She waved her mobile phone in front of her.

'You wouldn't!'

'No? Want to take the chance? You think I haven't

been *waiting* for an opportunity like this? Little miss goody-goody two shoes, making out you're soooo sweet and innocent.'

The boat bobbed further away from the jetty. 'Why do you hate me so much?' I called over the engine.

'Hmm. Let me think.' She put her finger dramatically to her mouth and looked away, as though talking to an audience. 'She gets me grounded, steals my best friend, turns the swimming teacher against me. She's a great big fat SHOW-OFF!' Mandy looked back at me. 'I really don't know.'

Then she turned and started walking back up the jetty, waving her phone in the air.

'Mandy, don't! Please!'

'Maybe I will, maybe I won't,' she called over her shoulder. 'See ya.'

What should I do? I couldn't go back. I *couldn't*. This was probably my one and only chance to find my father. And Mandy Rushton was NOT going to ruin it. I forced her words out of my mind. She wasn't going to stop me – she *wasn't!*

I turned my attention back to my plan.

Minutes later, I was edging away from the pier, holding the tiller and carefully navigating my way out of the harbour. I went over what I'd done when I drove the boat round to Southpool – and tried hard to convince myself that what I was doing now really wasn't very different.

As I sailed out to sea, I looked back at Brightport

Bay. The last rays of the sun winked and glinted on the water like tiny spotlights. Spray dusted my hair.

I closed my eyes for a second while I thought about what I was doing. I had to find the Great Mermer Reef. I knew more or less where it was, from the time we'd got halfway there, so I studied the horizon and aimed for the bit that was lighter than the rest. The bit that would shimmer a hundred colours when I got close.

It got dark quite suddenly as I sliced slowly through the water. *King* never does *anything* in a hurry. My hand was getting cold, holding onto the tiller. And I was getting wet. *King* bounced on the water, gliding along with the swell, then rising and bumping down over the waves. It had been quite calm when I set off. The further out I got, the more hill-like the sea became.

Above me, stars appeared, one by one. Soon, the night sky was packed. A fat half moon sat among them, its other half a silhouette, semi-visible as though impatient for the full moon to come.

King swayed from side to side, lumbering slowly through the peaks and troughs. Was I getting any-where? I looked behind me. Brightport was *miles* away! If I closed one eye and held up my hand, I could hide the whole town behind my thumbnail.

Up and down we went, climbing the waves, bouncing on the swell, inching ever closer to the Great Mermer Reef.

My eyes watered as I strained to keep them on the patch of light on the horizon, shimmering and glowing and coming gradually closer. I let myself dream about seeing Jake.

I'd get into the prison and we'd escape. Hiding him in the boat, we'd cruise back to the pier before anyone even realised he'd gone. Then Mum would come home from the meeting. Jake would be waiting in the sea at the end of the pier and I'd ask Mum to come for a walk with me. Then I'd leave her there on her own for a minute and he would appear. They'd see each other and it would be like they'd never been apart. Mum would remember everything and we'd all live happily ever after. *Excellent* plan.

Excellent daydream, anyhow. A 'plan' was something I didn't exactly have.

'EMILY!' A voice shattered my thoughts. I spun round, searching the night sky. There was a shape behind me – a long way away but coming nearer. A boat. One of those little motor boats with outboard engines that they hire out in the summer. As it got closer, I could see an outline of two people, one leaning forwards at the front, one at the back at the tiller.

'Emily!' A woman's voice. And not just any woman. Mum!

Then I recognised the other voice.

'Come back here, young lady! Whatever you think you are doing, you had better stop it – and *now!*'

Mr Beeston!

I shoved the tiller across and quickly swapped sides as the boat changed direction, pushing the throttle as far forward as it would go. *Come on, come on,* I snapped. The boat sputtered and chugged in reply but didn't speed up.

'What are you doing here?' I shouted, over the engine and the waves.

'What am *I* doing here?' Mum called back. 'Emily, what are YOU doing?'

'But your meeting!'

The motor boat edged closer. 'The meeting got cancelled when Mrs Rushton's girl rang up in a right state. She thought you might be in danger.'

I should have known she'd do it! I don't know how I could have thought even for a moment that she wouldn't.

'I'm sorry, Mum,' I called. 'I've got to do this. You'll understand, honestly. Trust me.'

'Oh, please come back, darling.' Mum called. 'Whatever it is, we can sort it out.'

King's engine sputtered again and seemed to be slowing down. Seawater soaked my face as we bounced on the waves, rolling and peaking like a mountain range.

'Look what you're doing to your mother,' Mr Beeston shouted. 'I won't have it, do you hear me? I won't allow it.'

I ran my sleeve over my wet face. 'You can't tell me what to do,' I shouted back, anger pushing away my fear – and any desire to keep my stupid promise to Mr Beeston. 'It's not like you're my father or anything.'

Mr Beeston didn't reply. He was concentrating hard and had almost caught up with me. Meanwhile, the shimmering light was glowing and growing bigger all the time. I could almost see the different colours. *Come on, King*, I said under my breath. *Not much further now*. I looked back at the motor boat. Mum was covering her face with her hands. Mr Beeston held the tiller tight, his face all pinched and contorted.

'*Remember* my father, do you?' I called to him. 'You know, your "best friend". What kind of a person lies to their best friend's wife for years then? *Huh?*'

'I don't know what foolish ideas you've got into your head, child, but you had better put an end to them right now. Before I put an end to them for you.' Mr Beeston's eyes shone like a cat's as he caught mine. 'Can't you see how much you are upsetting your mother?'

'Upsetting my mother? Ha! Like *you* care!'

'Emily, *please*,' Mum called, her arms stretched out towards me. 'Whatever it is, we'll talk about it. Don't blame Mr Beeston. He's only trying to help.'

'Come *on*, *King*!' I said out loud as the engine crackled and popped. 'Mum.' I turned to face her.

They were only a couple of metres away from me now. 'Mr Beeston isn't who he says he is. And he's *not* trying to help you.'

Then the engine died.

'What's the *matter* with this thing?' I shouted.

'You know we never keep much diesel on board,' Mum called. 'It's a fire hazard.'

'Fire hazard? Who told you that?'

'I did,' Mr Beeston called. 'Don't want you injuring yourselves, do I?' He smiled his creepy smile at me. He'd been controlling our whole lives!

That was it. I stood up and lurched forward to grab the mast. I'd have to sail the rest of the way!

I undid a rope at the base of the mast and tried to hoist the mainsail up. I heaved and yanked at it, but nothing happened. I pulled at another rope to free the boom – that's the wooden pole that runs along the bottom of the sail.

As the rope at the far end of the boom swung free, I made a grab for it. Missed. The sail swayed out to the side and I watched helplessly as my last hope swung away with it.

'Oh Emily, please stop it.' Mum shouted as the boat lurched to the side. 'You don't need to upset yourself like this. I know what it's about.'

'*What*? If you know, what are you doing in there with him?'

'It's natural for you to feel like this, darling. Mr Beeston's told me about you being a little jealous, and how that might make you try to turn me against him.

But he's just a friend. There's no need for you to go fretting like this.'

The shimmering was really close now. I could see colours and lights dancing on the surface of the water. It was like a fireworks display. I groaned. 'Mum, it's not –'

I broke off when I saw Mum's face. It had turned white, like those buskers in the market square who pretend to be statues. In a soft voice I hardly recognised, she said, 'No one could ever take the place of your father.' She was gazing wide-eyed at the lights on the water.

'*My father?*'

For a moment, everything stood completely still, like a picture. The sea stopped moving; Mr Beeston let go of the tiller; my mum and I locked eyes as though seeing each other for the first time.

Then Mr Beeston leapt into action. 'Right, that's it,' he yelled. 'I'm coming aboard.'

'Wait!' I shouted, as a wave caught the side of the boat. *King* lurched sideways, the sail swinging across to the other side.

Mr Beeston had just pulled himself aboard when – thwack! – the boom swung back again and knocked him flying.

'Aaarrrgghh!' He clutched his head as he fell backwards. Crashing to the deck with a thump, he lay flat on his back without moving.

Mum screamed and stood up. The motor boat rocked wildly.

'Mum – careful!' I ran to the side and leaned over. 'Get on,' I shouted. She was alongside *King*.

Mum didn't move.

'You have to get on board. Come on, Mum.' I held an arm out. 'I'll help you.'

'I – I can't,' she said woodenly.

'You can, Mum. You've *got* to.' I scrabbled around in the bench seat and pulled out the lifebelt. *King* rocked like the rodeo horse on the prom. The sail was still waving about at the side, hopelessly out of reach. Holding tight to the railing, I threw the lifebelt to Mum. 'You'll be fine,' I called. 'Just get on board quick before you drift away.'

She stared at me.

'*Do it!*'

Mum stood up in her rocky boat, the lifebelt round her middle, and suddenly lunged for the steps. I grabbed her hand as she pulled herself onto the deck.

'Oh Emily,' she said. 'I'm so sorry.'

'What for?'

'It's all my fault,' Mum said, holding onto me with one hand and the railing with the other as we swayed from side to side.

'Course it's not your fault, Mum. If it's anyone's fault, it's Mr Beeston's. He's not what he seems, Mum; he's been –'

Mum put her finger over my lips. 'I know why we're here.'

'You – you –'

'I remember.' Mum pulled me towards her and held me tight. Over her shoulder, I could see the water shimmering and sparkling like an electric light show. The Great Mermer Reef.

I wriggled out of Mum's grasp. 'You remember – what?'

Mum hesitated. 'It's all a bit hazy,' she said.

All at once, the sky exploded with light. 'Look!' I pointed behind her. Pink lights danced below the water while a dozen colours jumped in the air above it.

'I know this,' Mum said, her voice shaking. 'He – he brought me here.'

'Who? Mr Beeston?' I glanced nervously across at him. He still hadn't moved. Mum clutched the railing as the boat tilted again and I made my way over to join her. Her face was covered in spray from the sea. Except when I looked more closely, I realised it wasn't seawater at all. It was tears. 'Our first anniversary,' she said.

She'd been here with Jake?

'He told me where they would take him.'

'*Who* would take him?'

'If they ever found us out. He knew they'd get him in the end. We both knew it, but we couldn't stop. Because we loved each other so much.'

Mum's body sagged; I put my arms round her middle.

'I'm going to find him,' I said, holding her tighter. 'That's why I took the boat. I did it for all of us.'

134

'I can't bear it,' she said. 'I can remember every-thing. How could I have forgotten him? He was taken away because he loved me and I forgot all about him. How can I ever forgive myself?'

'Mum, it's not your fault! You didn't just *forget* him.'

'I did,' she gulped. 'You know I did. You asked about him and I didn't even know. I couldn't remem-ber anything.'

'But you weren't to blame.'

Mum wiped a curtain of wet hair off her face and looked at me. 'Who was, then?'

I nodded a thumb behind me. 'Mr Beeston,' I whispered.

'Oh, Emily. Don't start with that claptrap again!'

'It's NOT claptrap!' I tried to keep my voice down. I didn't want him to wake up and ruin everything. 'It's true,' I whispered. 'He's not what he seems.'

'Emily, please don't make this worse than it is.'

'Mum, *listen* to me,' I snapped.

She caught my eyes for a second. Then looked at Mr Beeston. 'We should see how he is.' Mum shook herself free from my grasp and stumbled along the deck to Mr Beeston.

'He'll be fine,' I said. 'Don't worry about him.'

Mum ignored me and crouched down next to Mr Beeston. I crouched down beside her as she leaned over his chest and listened. Then she looked up at me, her face whiter than the million stars shining above us.

'Oh my God,' she said. 'I think we've killed him.'

Chapter Twelve

'There's no heartbeat,' Mum said, rocking back on her heels.

I opened my mouth. What could I say? A second later, the side door suddenly swung open with a bang. Mum and I grabbed each other's arms.

Millie's face appeared in the doorway.

'Do you think there's anything you would like to share with me?' she asked as she hitched up her long skirt and clambered out onto the deck.

Mum and I looked at each other.

'I'm sensing some . . . disorientation.'

'No time now,' Mum said, beckoning Millie over. 'We have to do something. Mr Beeston has had an accident. I think he's dead.' She clapped a fist to her mouth.

Millie struggled over to join us, slipping and swaying on the wet deck. 'Let's have a look,' she said, kneeling down beside Mr Beeston. She undid his coat and lifted up his jumper. He was wearing a thick, padded jacket of some sort underneath. I flinched as I noticed a picture of Neptune's trident sewn onto a pocket.

'Armoured vest?' Millie murmured. 'Now why in the cosmos would he need something like that?'

I didn't say anything.

'That's your answer, Mary P.' Millie turned to Mum. 'You wouldn't hear a ten ton truck through that.'

Just then, the boat jolted to the side. I slid across the deck and bumped against the bench seat.

'Emily, get the tiller!' Millie ordered, suddenly in charge.

I did what she said, not that it made much difference. The boat dipped and swayed helplessly in the waves.

Millie reached under Mr Beeston's back and unbuckled the vest. Lifting it off, she bent over him, her ear to his chest. Mum came over and grabbed my hand while we waited.

'Absolutely fine,' Millie announced a few seconds later.

'Oh thank heavens.' Mum hugged me. 'I'd never have forgiven myself if anything had happ–'

'He just needs his chakras realigning,' Millie continued. 'A bit of reflexology should do it.'

She pulled off his shoes and socks and settled herself at Mr Beeston's feet. Placing her hands across her large chest, she closed her eyes and breathed in deeply. Then she lifted his right foot and started to massage it. A moment later, his foot twitched. She carried on massaging. He twitched again, this time his leg jerking about in the air. The twitching and jerking spread up his body until it reached his face and he started giggling. He was soon laughing loudly. Eventually, he leapt up, screaming, 'Stop, stop!'

Millie released his foot and stood up. 'Never fails,' she said, wiping her hands on her skirt and heading back inside. 'Right, give me a minute or two. Reflexology always drains my chi.'

Mum went over to Mr Beeston. 'Thank heavens you're all right.'

Mr Beeston straightened his coat as he glanced at me. 'Just a scratch,' he said. 'No harm done.' A red path was worming its way down the side of his head.

My hand tightened on the tiller. 'No harm done? You *reckon*?'

'Emily, this is no time to start your nonsense again. What on *earth* have you got against the poor man?'

'What have I got against the poor man? Where d'you want me to start?' I looked him in the eyes. 'Is it the fact that he's been wiping your memory since the day I was born, or the fact that he's been spying on us *forever*?'

Mum didn't speak for a second. Then she laughed. 'Oh Emily, I've never heard such –'

'It's true.' Mr Beeston spoke, his eyes still locked onto mine. 'She's right.'

'What?' Mum held tightly onto the mast with one hand; with the other, she clutched her chest.

'It's too late, Mary P. I can't pretend any more. And I won't. Why should I?'

'What are you *on* about?' Mum looked from Mr Beeston to me. Let *him* explain.

Mr Beeston sat down on the bench opposite me. 'It was for your own good,' he said. 'All of you.' His hands were still clutching his head, his hair all mangled and tangled up with blood and sweat and seawater.

'What was for my own good?' Mum's face hardened and grew thinner as she spoke.

'The two worlds – they don't belong together. It doesn't work.' He leant forward, his head almost between his knees. 'And I should know,' he added, his voice almost a whisper. 'You're not the only one to grow up without a father.' He spoke to the floor. 'Disappeared the minute I was born, he did. Just like all the others. Fishermen. All very nice having an unusual girlfriend isn't it? Taming a beautiful siren. Show off to your friends about that, can't you?'

A tear fell from his face onto the deck. He brushed his cheek roughly. 'But it's a bit different when your

139

own son sprouts a tail! Don't want to know, then, do you?'

'What are you saying?' Mum's voice was as tight as her face, her hand still gripping the mast. The sea lifted us up and down; the sail still flapped uselessly over the water.

'You can't put humans and merfolk together and expect it to work. It doesn't. All you get is pain.' Finally, Mr Beeston raised his head to look at us. 'I was trying to save you from that. From what I've been through, myself.'

The boat shook violently as another wave hit us. I clutched the tiller more tightly. 'I told you he wasn't really your friend,' I hissed to Mum, the wind biting my face.

'Friendship?' he spat. 'Loyalty is all that matters. To Neptune and the protection of the species. That is my life.' He held up a fist across his chest. Then he glanced at Mum. His fist fell open. 'That's to say,' he faltered, 'I mean – look, I never wanted to . . . ' His voice trailed away, his chin dropping to his chest.

Mum looked like she'd been hit over the head herself. Her face was as white as the sail and her body had gone rigid. 'I often wondered why they got a new lighthouse keeper so suddenly,' she said. 'No one ever did quite explain what happened to old Bernard. You just appeared one day. And something else I've never really thought about – you never invited me in. Not once in twelve years. Not like Bernard. We used to go up there all the time when I was younger, up on the top deck looking all round with binoculars and telescopes. But you – my *friend* – you always kept the door closed to me. And to think, I actually felt sorry for you.'

She put her hand on my arm. The boat was starting to career up and down, the sea getting wilder as we held the tiller together. 'He saw you once,' she said quietly into the darkness. 'At Rainbow Rocks. Held you against his chest at the water's edge. I wouldn't let him take you in the water. Maybe if he had. . .' Her words slipped away as she looked at me, her hair plastered across her face with sea water. 'Twelve years I've lost.'

I bit my lip, tasting salty water.

'Hidden from my own mind like everything else.' She stood up and inched over towards Mr Beeston. 'You stole my life from me,' she said, anger creeping into her voice. 'You're nothing but a thief! A nasty, rotten, scheming THIEF!'

'Hey now, hold on a minute!' Mr Beeston stood up. 'I've been *good* to you. I've looked *after* you. You should hear what some of them wanted to –'

'You had no right.' Mum shook his arm, tears rolling down her cheeks. 'He is my husband. Who do you think you are?'

'Who do I think I am? I know *exactly* who I am! I'm Charles – ' He stopped. Glanced briefly at Mum and took a breath. Then he suddenly thrust out his chin, his eyes clear and focused for a brief moment. 'I am Charles Finright Beeston, adviser to Neptune, and I have conducted my duties with pride and loyalty for twelve years.'

'How dare you!' Mum snapped. 'All these years, pretending to be my friend.'

'Now wait a minute. I was – I mean, I *am* your friend. You think I didn't care about you? It's for your own good. We had to put a stop to it. It's wrong, unnatural – dangerous, even – don't you see?'

Mum paused for a moment, then flew at him, bashing her fists against his chest. 'All I can see is a beast. A despicable worm!' she screamed.

Mr Beeston backed away from her. As she went for him, Mum tripped on the lifebelt and nearly fell flat on her face. She stopped herself by clutching a rope tied onto the mast. The rope came loose in her hand, ripping the canvas that held the boom in place. All three of us watched as the wooden plank drifted away from us and the sail flapped over the sea even more uselessly than before.

We'd *never* get anywhere now.

I tried to hold the tiller steady as the boat lurched again. The waves were getting choppier, throwing us all over the deck. 'We need to do something,' I said, my voice quivering.

'I'll fix it,' Mr Beeston said, his words slow and deliberate, his eyes cold and determined. Then he turned and walked along the side of the boat to the door, holding the railing as the boat rocked.

'Mum, what are we going to do?' I asked as the waves rolled us from side to side again. Mum's steely eyes followed Mr Beeston down the boat.

'Forget him,' I said. 'We need to think of something or we'll never get home again – never mind see Jake.'

'Oh Emily, do you really think we're going to find –'

'I know where he is,' I said. 'We can do it. We're nearly there!'

Mum pulled her eyes away from Mr Beeston. 'Right. Come on,' she said, snapping into action. She lifted the lid up off the bench, rummaged through hose pipes and foot pumps. 'Put this on.' She passed me a lifejacket that was much too small for me and grabbed one for herself.

'Mum. I don't need one.'

'Just to be on the safe –' She stopped and looked at my legs. 'Oh golly,' she said. 'You mean you can . . . you're a –'

'Didn't you know?' I asked. 'Didn't you ever suspect?'

She shook her head sadly. 'How could I have done? Maybe somewhere in the back of my mind . . . ' A massive wave crashed over the side, washing away the rest of her sentence and drenching us both.

'Mum, I'm scared,' I yelped, wiping the spray off my face. 'It's too far even for me to swim back from here. We'll never make it.'

As I spoke, the boat gave one more enormous lurch to the side. I fell to the floor, slipped across the deck. As I clutched the railing and tried to pull myself up again, I noticed a shape in the sea in front of us. A fin! That was it, then. The boat was going to capsize; we'd be eaten by sharks!

Mum has never been religious and she's always said it's up to me to make my mind up. I never had done. Until then.

Without even wondering what to say, I put my hands together, closed my eyes and prayed.

Chapter Thirteen

*M*y lips moved soundlessly behind my hands, scanning all the words I could summon up: half-remembered prayers from half-listened-to assemblies. *Why didn't I take more notice?* I asked myself when I got to, 'Thy will be done on earth as it is in heaven,' and couldn't for the life of me think what came next.

'*Emily!*' Mum was tugging at my arm.

I shook her off. 'I'm busy.'

Mum tugged again. 'I think you should take a look.'

I opened my fingers wide enough to sneak a peek between them. It was hard to see anything, the boat was careering up and down so much. I felt even more giddy and reached out for the railing. That was when

I heard it — someone calling my name! I looked at Mum even though I knew it hadn't been her. Holding the railing beside me, she pointed out to the mountainous waves with her free hand.

'Emily!' a familiar voice called again. Then a familiar head poked out above the waves, bobbing up and down in the swell. Shona! She grinned and waved at me.

'What are you doing here?' I shouted.

'It's Monday. You didn't turn up at the rocks. I've been looking for you.'

'Oh Shona, I'm so sorry.'

'When you didn't come, I had a funny feeling you'd be doing something like this!'

'I've messed it all up,' I called, my throat clogged up. 'We're never going to get there now.'

'Don't be too sure!' she called back. 'Throw me a rope. I'll see if I can tow you.'

'But the boat must weigh a ton!'

'Not in water it doesn't. As long as I can get some momentum going with my tail. We do it in PE all the time.'

'Are you sure?'

'Let's just give it a try, OK?'

'OK,' I said uncertainly, and with a flick of her tail, she was gone. Her tail! Of course! Not a shark at all!

I made my way up to the front deck, untied the rope and threw it down. Mum came with me. I tried to avoid looking at her but I could feel her eyes boring into the side of my face. 'What?' I asked without turning to her.

'Is she a . . . friend of yours?' Mum asked carefully.

'Mm.'

Mum sighed. 'We've got a lot of catching up to do, love, haven't we?'

I carried on looking ahead. 'Do you think I'm a freak?'

'A freak?' Mum reached over to pick up one of my hands. 'Darling, I couldn't be more proud.'

Still holding my hand, she put her other arm round me. The boat had levelled out again and I snuggled into Mum's shoulder; wet, cold and frightened. Neither of us spoke for a few minutes while we watched Shona pull us ever nearer to the prison – and Jake.

A few moments later, Mum and I caught each other's eyes, the same thought coming into our minds. *Where was Mr Beeston?*

'He might be hiding,' Mum said.

'I think we should check it out.'

Mum stood up. 'I'll go then.'

'I'm coming with you.'

She didn't argue as we stood up and edged our way down the side of the boat. The deck was still soaking and it was a slippy trip to the door.

I pushed my head inside. Mr Beeston was standing by a window in the saloon, his back to us, the window pushed open, a large shell in his hands.

'A conch? What on earth is he doing with that?' Mum whispered.

Mr Beeston put the shell to his mouth.

'Talking to it?' I whispered back.

He muttered quietly into the shell.

'What's he saying?' I looked at Mum.

She shook her head. 'Stay here,' she ordered. 'Crouch down behind the door. Don't let him see you. I'll be back in a second.'

'Where are you going?' But she'd slid back outside. I hunched low and waited for her to return.

Two minutes later, Mum was back with a huge fishing net in her arms. 'What are you doing with –'

Mum shushed me with a finger over her lips and crept inside. She beckoned me to follow.

Mr Beeston was still leaning out of the window, talking softly into his conch. Mum inched towards him and I tiptoed behind her. When we were right behind him, she passed me one end of the net and mouthed, 'Three . . . two . . . '

When she mouthed, 'One,' I threw my side of the net over Mr Beeston's head. Mum did the same on her side.

'What the – ' Mr Beeston dropped the conch and fell back into a chair.

'Quick, wrap it round him,' Mum urged.

I ran in a circle round him, dragging the net with me. Mr Beeston struggled and lashed out but we wrapped him up, like when someone's dog runs up to you in the park and knots your ankles together with its lead. Only better.

Mum pushed him back into his chair and lifted his

legs up. 'Get his feet,' she demanded, dodging his kicks. I slipped under his legs with the net. There was still loads of net left over so I ran round him again, fastening him to his chair. Mum grabbed my end of the net and tied it securely to hers and we stood back to admire our work.

'You won't get away with this, you know,' Mr Beeston said, struggling and trying to kick out. All he managed to do was make the chair wobble on its legs.

'I wouldn't do that if I were you,' a voice suddenly boomed from the other side of the saloon.

We all turned to see Millie clambering up off the sofa. She stood majestically in the centre of the room, arms raised as though waiting for a voice from heaven.

'Put my back out for weeks once, falling backwards off a chair. Had to see a chiropractor for six months. And they're not cheap, I can tell you.' She swept into the galley. 'Right, who's for an Earl Grey?' she asked. 'I'm gasping.'

The sea had calmed down and we drank our tea on the front deck. The sky sparkled with dancing colours. As we watched, the lights danced faster and faster. Pink, blue, green, gold – every colour you could imagine, in a million different shades, jumping around, stabbing at the water as though it was too hot for them to settle. It was as if the lights were speaking – in an alien language that I had no chance of understanding.

Millie looked at them intently for a while, then sniffed her cup of tea. 'I don't know what they put in this,' she said, draining the cup and heading back inside, 'but I'll have to get some in.'

Mum buttoned up her coat, her eyes fixed on the lights.

'All of this,' she whispered. 'I remember it all.'

'Do you remember Jake?' I asked nervously, remembering what happened last time I tried to find out about him.

'We never meant it to happen,' she said, her eyes misting over. 'He told me right from the start how dangerous it would be. It was after the regatta.'

'The regatta?'

'We used to hold it every year, but that was the last one. I don't know how we went so wrong, but we did. I went with Mrs Brighouse who used to run the Sea View B & B. She had a little two-man yacht. We got into trouble on the rocks. That was when I met Jake.' She looked at me for the first time. 'Your father,' she added, before looking away again. 'I don't know what happened to Mrs Brighouse. She moved away soon afterwards. But Jake and I – well, I couldn't help it. I went back to Rainbow Rocks every night.'

'*Rainbow Rocks?*'

'Well, near enough. I waited by those rocks you took me to. You know?'

'Yes. I know.'

She smiled sadly. 'You knew more than I did. But not any more. I remember it all.'

'So did he come?'

She shook her head. 'I waited every night. Then one night I told myself I'd give it one last try before giving up for good. I just wanted to thank him.' She turned to face me again. 'He saved my life, Emily.'

'And he came?'

She smiled. 'He'd been there every night.'

'Every night? But you said – '

'He hid. He saw me every time I went. Said he couldn't keep away either, but he couldn't bring himself to talk to me.'

'Why not?'

'You know, that first time, when he helped us . . . he never got out of the water.' Mum laughed. 'I thought at the time, what an amazing swimmer!'

'So you didn't know . . .'

'He thought I'd be shocked, or disgusted or something.'

I took a deep breath. 'And were you?'

Mum put her hand out to me, cupped my chin. 'Emily, when I saw his tail, when I knew what he was – I think that was the moment I fell in love with him.'

'Really?'

She smiled. 'Really.'

'So then what happened?'

'Well, that was when I left home.'

'Left home? You mean Nan and Grandad used to live here?'

Mum swallowed hard. 'I remember why we argued, now. They wouldn't believe me. They thought I was mad. Tried to make me see a psychiatrist.'

'And you wouldn't.'

She shook her head. 'So then they sold up and moved away from the sea. They gave me an ultimatum – either I came with them, or . . .'

'Or they didn't want to know.' I finished her sentence for her.

'The boat was your grandad's. He didn't want anything more to do with it – or me. Said he'd had enough of the sea to last him a lifetime.'

'He gave it to you?'

She nodded. 'I like to think the gesture meant that a part of him knew it was true. Knew I wasn't crazy.'

'And what about Jake?'

'I used to sail out to sea to meet him, or round to Rainbow Rocks.'

'Was that where they caught him?'

She dabbed the edge of her eye with the palm of her hand. 'I never believed it would happen,' she said. 'Somehow, I thought everything would be all right. Especially after you were born.'

'How come they didn't make you move away?'

'Maybe they wanted to keep an eye on us.'

'On me, you mean?'

She pulled me close, hugging me tight. 'Oh Emily,' she whispered into my hair. 'You only saw him once. You were so tiny.'

'I'm going to see him again, Mum,' I said, my voice coming out in a squeak. 'I'm going to find him.'

She smiled at me through misty eyes.

'I *am*.'

A moment later, I noticed Shona swimming round to the side of the boat. 'We're nearly there,' she called. 'Are you coming in?'

I looked at Mum. 'Is it OK?' I asked.

For an answer, she pulled me tighter – then let me go.

I ran inside and changed into my swimming costume. Millie came back out with me. I perched on the edge of the boat. 'See you,' I smiled.

Mum swallowed hard and held Millie's hand as I jumped into the water. Within seconds I felt my tail form. My legs melted and stretched, spreading warmth through my whole body. I waved to Mum and Millie, watching me from the front deck.

'Look!' I shouted, then ducked under the water. I flicked my tail as gracefully as I could, waving it from side to side while I stretched out in a downwards handstand. When I came back up, Mum was clapping. 'Beautiful,' she called, wiping something from her eye. She blew me a kiss as I grinned at her. Millie's eyes widened. She shook her head, then picked up Mum's cup of tea and finished that one off as well.

'Are you ready?' Shona asked.

'As I'll ever be,' I replied and we set off.

The Great Mermer Reef isn't like anything you are ever likely to see in your life. The highest, widest, longest wall in the world – in the universe, probably – made out of rainbow-coloured coral, miles and miles from anywhere. In the middle of the sea.

You don't realise what it is at first. It feels like the end of the world, stretching up and down and across, further than you can see in every direction. I shielded my eyes from the brightness. It reminded me of the school disco we had at the end of last term. They'd borrowed this machine that threw lights across the room, swirling around and changing colour in time to the music. The Great Mermer Reef was a bit like that, but about a million times bigger and brighter, and the colours swirled and flashed even more.

And somehow, we had to get past it! It was the only way to the prison.

As we got closer, the swirling lights became laser beam rays, shooting out at every angle from jagged layers of coral heaped upon coral.

Sharp, spiky rocks were piled all the way up to the surface – and higher – with soft, rubbery bushes buried in every crevice in the brightest purples and yellows and greens you've ever seen. A moving bush like a silver Christmas tree flapped towards us. Two spotted shrimps dragged a starfish along the seabed. All around us, fish and plants bustled and rustled about. But we were stuck – in a fortress of bubbles and bushes and rocks. We couldn't even climb over the top; it was far too high and rough. Above the water, the coral shot diamond rays from stones like cut glass. I was never, *ever* going to find Jake.

'It's hopeless,' I said, trying desperately not to cry. It was like that stupid game about going on a bear hunt. You keep coming across things that you've got to get past. 'We can't get over it, we can't get under it.'

Shona was by my side, her eyes bright like the coral. 'We'll have to go through it!' she exclaimed, her words gurgling away in multicoloured bubbles. 'There's bound to be a gap somewhere. Come on.' She pulled at my arm and dived deeper.

We weaved in and out of spaghetti-fringed tubes, swam into bushes with tentacles that opened wide enough to swim inside. But it was the same thing every time: a dead end.

I perched on a rock, ready to give up, while Shona scaled the coral, tapping it with her fingers like a builder testing the thickness of a wall. A huge shoal of fish that had been sheltering in a cave suddenly darted out as one, writhing and spinning like a kaleidoscope pattern. I stared, transfixed.

'I think I've found something.' Shona's voice jolted me out of my trance. She was scratching about at the coral and I swam closer to see what she'd found.

'Look!' She scrabbled some more. Bits of coral crumbled away like dust in her fingers. She pulled me round and made me look closer. 'What can you see?' she asked.

'I can't see anything.'

'Look harder.'

'What at?'

Shona pushed her face close to mine and pointed into the jagged hole she'd scraped away at. She pushed her fist into it and pulled out some more dust; it floated away, dancing round us as she scraped.

'It's a weak point,' she said. 'This stuff's millions of years old. I'm sure they have people who check the perimeter and maintain it and stuff, but there's always going to be a bit of it that they miss.'

I pushed my own hand into the hole, scrabbled at it with my fingertips as though I was digging a hole into sand. It felt different from the rest of the wall. Softer. I pushed further.

Scrabbling and scraping, we'd soon scooped all the way up to our shoulders, white dust clouds billowing around us.

'Now what?' I asked.

'Make it wider. Big enough to swim into.'

We worked silently at the hole. The coral didn't glint and glisten with colours once we got inside it. We scraped and scratched in darkness.

Eventually, as my arms were going numb and my whole body was aching and itching from the dust particles swirling all around us, Shona grabbed my arm. I looked up and saw it. The tiniest flicker of light ahead of us.

'We're through,' I gasped.

'Nearly. Come on.'

Filled with hope, I punched my fist deep into the hole, scratching my hand as I pulled at the wall. The hole grew bigger and rounder, eventually large enough to get through. I turned to Shona.

'Go on. You first,' she urged. 'You're smaller than me.'

I scrunched my arms tightly against my body and flicked my tail gently. Then, scratching my arms and tail on the sides, I slid through the hole.

Once on the other side, I turned and carried on scraping so Shona could get through as well. But nothing came away in my hands. No dust. I cut my fingers against jagged rock.

'I can't make it bigger,' I called through the hole.

'Me neither,' Shona replied, her voice echoing inside the dark cavern I'd left behind.

'Try to squeeze through.'

Shona's head came close to the hole. 'It's my shoulders. I'm too big,' she said. 'I'll never manage it.'

'Shall I pull you?'

'I can't do it.' Shona backed away from the gap. 'I'll get stuck – and then you won't be able to get back through.'

'I can't do it without you.' My voice shook as it rippled through the water to her.

'I'll wait here.'

'Promise?'

'I'll wait at the end of the tunnel.'

I took a deep breath. 'This is it then,' I said, poking my head into the opening.

'Good luck.'

'Yeah.' I backed away from the hole again. 'And thanks,' I added. 'For everything. You're the bestest best friend anyone could want.'

Shona's eyes shone brighter in the darkness. '*You* are, you mean.'

There was *no way* I'd been as good a friend as she had. I didn't tell her that, though – didn't want her to change her mind!

Then I turned away from the hole. Leaving the Great Mermer Reef behind me, I swam towards a dark maze of caves covered in sharp, jagged pieces of coral.

'I'm going to see my dad,' I whispered, trying out the unfamiliar thought, and desperately hoping it could be true.

Chapter Fourteen

I swam cautiously away from the reef, glancing nervously around me as I moved ever closer to the prison. A solitary manta ray slid along the ground, flapping its fins like a cape. Small packs of moody-looking fish with open jaws threaded slowly through the silent darkness, glancing at me as they passed. Ahead of me, a barrel of thick blackness rotated slowly. Then suddenly, it parted! Thousands of tiny fish scattered and reformed into two spinning balls. Beyond them, a dark grey shadow, bigger than me and shaped like a submarine, moved silently between them.

I held my breath as the shark passed by.

As I drew nearer to the prison, the water grew darker. Dodging between rocks and weeds, I finally reached the prison door. It looked like the wide-open mouth of a gigantic whale, with sharp white teeth filling the gap. In front of the door, two creatures silently glided from side to side. Slow and mean with a beady eye on each side of their mallet-shaped heads. Hammerhead sharks.

I'd *never* get past them. Maybe there was another entrance.

I remembered the note in Dad's file. 'East Wing,' it had said. Shame there wasn't one of those *You are here* signs, like you get in big shopping centres.

I figured I'd been heading west since I'd set off as I'd been chasing the setting sun all the way. We'd turned right to head towards the reef. Which meant I should now be facing north.

I turned right again. In front of me was a long tunnel attached to the main cave. It reminded me of those service stations on the motorway – the bit that joins the two sides together. Apart from the fact that this was made of rock, didn't appear to have any windows and was about fifty feet under the sea. The East Wing?

Swimming carefully from one lump of coral to another and hiding behind every rock I could find, I made it to the tunnel. But there was no entrance. I swam all the way along it, right to the end. Still no opening.

The front gate must be the only way in. I'd come all this way for nothing! There was *no way* I'd get past those sharks.

I started to swim back along the other side of the tunnel. Perhaps there'd be a doorway on this side.

But as I made my way along the slimy walls, I heard a swishing noise behind me. The sharks! Without stopping to think, I flicked my tail and zoomed straight down so I was underneath the tunnel itself. Pressing myself up against the wall, I wrapped a huge piece of seaweed round my body. Two hammerheads sliced past without stopping and I inched my way back up again, scaling the edge with my hands and looking around me all the way. A minute later, I noticed something I hadn't seen earlier. A gap. An oval shape about half my height and slightly wider than my shoulders with three thick, grey bars running down it. They looked like whale bones. The nearest thing I'd found to a way in – it had to be worth a try.

I tugged at the bars. Rock solid. I tried to swim between them. I could get my head through, but my shoulders were too big to follow. This wasn't going to work.

Unless I swam through on my side...

I tried again, coming at the bars sideways on. But it was no good. I couldn't squeeze my face through the gap. I never realised my nose stuck out that much!

I held onto the bars, flicking my tail as I thought. Then it hit me. How could I have been so stupid? I turned to face them. Just like before, I edged my head through the bars, as slowly and carefully as I could. All I needed to do now was flip onto my side and pull the rest of my body through.

But what if I got stuck – my head on one side, my body on the other, caught forever with my neck in these railings?

Before I had time to talk myself out of it, I swivelled my body onto its side. I banged my chin, and my neck rubbed on the bars – but I'd done it! I swished my tail as gently as possible and gradually eased my body through the gap.

I thought back to the time when we were changing to go swimming and how I hadn't wanted anyone to see my skinny body. Maybe being a little weed wasn't such a bad thing, after all.

I rubbed my eyes as I got used to the darkness. I'd landed in a tiny round bubble of a room full of seaweed mops hanging on fish hooks all around me.

I swam to the door and turned a yellow knob. The door creaked open. Which way? The corridor was a long, narrow cave. Closing the door behind me, I noticed a metal plate in the top corner. 'NW: N 874' North Wing? I must have got my calculations wrong!

I swam along the silent corridor, passing closed doors on either side. N 867, N 865. Each one the same. A big round plate of metal, like a submarine door, a brass knob below a tiny round window in the centre. No glass, just fishbone bars dividing each window into an empty game of noughts and crosses.

Should I look?

As I approached the next door, I swished up to the window and peeked in. A merman with a huge hairy stomach and long black hair in a pony tail swam over to the window. 'Can I help you?' he asked, an amused glint in his eye. He had a ship tattooed on his arm; a fat brown tail flickered behind him.

'Sorry!' I flipped myself over and darted away. This was impossible! I wasn't even in the right wing. And there were scary criminals behind those doors! Which was only to be expected, I suppose. This was a prison, after all.

Suddenly, I heard a swooshing noise. Hammer-heads! Coming nearer. I flicked my tail as hard as I could and swam to the end of the corridor. I had to get round the bend before they saw me!

With one last push of my tail, I zoomed round the corner – into an identical tunnel.

Identical except for one thing. The numbers all started with 'E'. The East Wing!

I swam carefully up to the first door. E 924. I tried to remember the number from that note in Mr Beeston's files. Why hadn't I written it down?

An old merman with a beard and a raggedy limp tail was inside the cell, facing away from me. I moved on. E 926, E 928. Would I ever find him?

Just then, two mallet-shaped heads appeared round the corner. I hurled myself up against the next door, frantically twisting the brass knob. To my amazement, it wasn't locked! The door swung open. Banking on the odds that whoever occupied it would be less scary than the sharks, I backed into the room and quietly shut the door. The whooshing noise came past the moment I'd closed it. I leaned my head against the door in relief.

'That was a lucky escape.'

Who said that? I swung round to see a merman sitting on the edge of a bed made of seaweed. He was leaning over a small table, his sparkly purple tail flickering gently.

'What are you doing?' I didn't move from the door.

He put the end of a piece of thread in his mouth and tied a knot in the other end. 'Got to keep myself busy somehow,' he said.

I slunk round the edges of the bubble-shaped room. The thread looked as if it was made of gold. Beads or something on it. Rainbow colours.

'You're making a necklace?'

'Bracelet, actually. Got a problem with that?' The merman looked up for the first time and I backed away instinctively. Don't make fun of criminals whose cells you've just barged into, I told myself. Never a good idea if you're planning to get out again in one piece.

Except he didn't look like a criminal. Not how you

imagine a criminal to look, anyhow. He didn't look mean and hard. And he *was* making jewellery. He had short black hair; kind of wavy, a tiny sleeper in one ear. A white vest with a blue prison jacket over it. His tail sparkled as much as the bracelet. As I looked at him, he ran his hand through his hair. There was something familiar about the way he did it, although I couldn't think what. I twiddled with my hair as I tried to –

I looked harder at him. As he squinted back at me, I noticed a tiny dimple appear. *Below his left eye.*

It couldn't be . . .

The merman put his bracelet down and slithered off his bed. I backed away again as he came towards me. 'I'll scream,' I said.

He stared at me. I stared back.

'How did you find me?' he said, in a different kind of voice from earlier. This one sounded like he had treacle blocking up his throat or something.

I looked into his face. Deep brown eyes. My eyes.

'Dad?' a tiny voice squeaked from over the other side of the cell somewhere.

The merman rubbed his eyes. Then he hit himself on the side of the head. 'Knew it would happen one day,' he said, to himself more than me. 'No one does a stretch in this place without going a little bit crazy.' He turned away from me. 'Dreaming, that's all.'

Then he turned back round. 'Pinch me,' he said, swimming closer. I recoiled a little.

'Pinch me,' he repeated.

I pinched him and he jumped back. 'Youch! Didn't say pull my skin off.' He rubbed his arm before looking up at me again. 'So you're real?' he said.

I nodded.

He swam in a circle around me. 'You're even more beautiful than I'd dreamed,' he said. 'And I've dreamed about you a lot, I can tell you.'

I still couldn't speak.

'Never wanted you to see me in this place.' He swam around his cell, tidying his jewellery things away. He picked some magazines up off the floor and shoved them into a crack in the wall; threw a vest under his bed. 'No place for a young girl.'

Then he swam back, came really close to me; held his hand up to my face and I forced myself not to move.

He cradled the side of my face in his palm, stroked my dimple with his thumb, wiped the tears away as they mingled with the seawater.

'Emily,' he whispered. It *was* him. My dad!

A second later, he was holding me in his strong arms and I clutched him as tightly as I could. 'A mermaid as well,' he murmured into my hair.

'Only some of the time,' I said.

'Figures.'

He loosened his arms and held me away from him. 'Where's your mother?' he asked suddenly. 'Is she here? Is she all right?' He dropped his arms to his sides. 'Has she met someone else?'

I inched closer to him. 'Of course she hasn't met anyone else!'

'My Penny,' he smiled.

'*Penny*?'

'My lucky penny. S'what I always called her. Guess it wasn't too accurate in the end.' Then he smiled. 'But she hasn't forgotten me?'

'Um.' How was I meant to answer that! 'She still loves you.' Well, she did, didn't she? She must do or she wouldn't have been so upset when she remembered everything. 'And she hasn't *really* forgotten you – at least, not any more.'

'Not any more?'

'Listen. I'll tell you everything.' And I did. I told him about the memory drugs and Mr Beeston and about what happened when I took Mum to Rainbow Rocks. And about our journey to the Great Mermer Reef.

'So she's here?' he broke in. 'She's that close?'

I nodded. He flattened his hair down, spun round in circles, swam away from me.

'Dad.' *Dad! I still couldn't get used to that*. 'She's waiting for me. She can't get into the prison.' I followed him over to his table. 'She can't swim,' I added softly.

He burst out laughing as he turned to face me. 'Can't swim? What are you on about? She's the smoothest, sleekest swimmer you could find – excluding mermaids, of course.'

My mum? A smooth, sleek swimmer? I laughed.

'I guess that disappeared along with the memory,' he said sadly. 'We swam all over. She even took sub aqua lessons so she could join me underwater. Went to that old shipwreck. That's where I proposed, you know.'

'She still loves you,' I said again.

'Yeah.' He swam over to the table by his bed. I followed him.

'What's this?' I asked. There was something pinned onto the wall with a fish hook. A poem.

'That's me, that is,' he said miserably.

'"The Forsaken Merman"?' I read. I scanned the lines, not taking any of it in – until I came to one that made me gasp out loud. *A ceiling of amber, a pavement of pearl.*

'But that's, but that's – '

'Yeah, I know. Soppy old stuff, isn't it.'

'No! I know those lines.'

Jake looked up at me. 'You been to that shipwreck yourself, little 'un?'

I nodded. 'Shona took me. My friend. She's a mermaid.'

'And your mother?'

'No – she doesn't even know *I've* been there.'

Jake dropped his head.

'But she knows those lines!' I said.

I pulled the poem off the wall, reading on. 'She left lonely for ever the kings of the sea,' I said out loud.

'That's how it ends,' he said.

'But it's not!'

'Not what?'

'That's not how it ends!'

168

'It does; look here.' Jake swam over, took the poem from me. 'Those are the last lines.'

I snatched it back. 'But that's not how *your* story ends! She never left the king of the sea!'

Jake scratched his head. 'You've lost me now.'

'*The King of the Sea*. That's our boat! That's what it's called.'

His eyes went all misty like Mum's had earlier. 'So it is, love. I remember when we renamed it. I forget what her father had called it before that. But you see –'

'And she could never leave it! She told me that. And now I know why. Because it's you! She could never leave you! You're not the forsaken merman at all!'

Jake laughed. 'You really think so?' Then he pulled me close again. He smelt of salt. His chin was bristly against my forehead.

'Look – you'll need to go soon,' he said, holding me away from him.

'But I've only just found you!'

'Dinner bell rings soon. We need to get you out of here. I don't know how you got your way into this place, little gem, but you sure as sharks don't want to get caught here. Might never get out again.'

'Don't you want me?'

He held my hands and looked deep into my eyes, locking us into a world of our own. 'I want you alive,' he said. 'I want you free, and happy. I don't want you slammed up in some stupid place like this for the rest of your life.'

'I'll never see you again,' I said.

'We'll find a way, little gem.' I liked him calling me that. 'Come on,' he said, looking quickly from side to side. 'We need to get you out of here.' He opened his door and looked down into the corridor.

'How come you can do that?' I asked. 'Aren't you meant to be locked up in here?'

He pointed to a metal tag stapled to the end of his tail.

'Does that hurt?'

'Keeps me in my place. Take it across the threshold,' he pointed at the doorway, 'and I know about it. Like being slammed between two walls.'

'Have you tried it?'

He rubbed his head as though he'd just bashed it. 'Not to be advised, I tell you.'

I giggled. 'Why *have* doors then?'

He shrugged. 'Extra security – they lock 'em at night.' He swam back towards me. 'You understand, don't you?'

'I think so.' I suddenly remembered Mr Beeston's words, how he said my dad ran off because he didn't want to be saddled with a baby. But Mr Beeston had lied about *everything*. Hadn't he?

'What is it, little 'un?'

I looked down at my tail, flicking rapidly from side to side. ' It's not that you didn't want me?' I said.

'*What?*' He swam over to his bed. I'd totally scared him off. I wished I could I take the words back.

He reached under the bed. 'Look at this.' He

170

pulled a pile of plastic papers out. 'Take a look. Any of them.'

I approached him shyly. 'Go on,' he urged. 'Have a look.' He passed me one. It was a poem. I read it aloud.

'"I never thought I'd see the day,

They'd take my bonny bairn away.

I long-ed for her every day.

Alas, she is so far away.'

'Yeah, well, it was an early one,' he said, pulling at the sleeper in his ear. 'There's better than that in here.'

I couldn't take my eyes off the poem. 'You . . .'

'Yeah, I know. Jewellery, poetry. What next, eh?' He pulled a face.

Before I could say anything else, a bell started ringing. It sounded like the school fire alarm. I clapped my hands over my ears.

'That's it. Dinner. They'll be here soon.' He grabbed me. 'Emily. You have to go.'

'Can I keep it?' I asked.

He folded the poem up and handed it back to me. Then he held my arms tightly. 'I'll find you,' he said roughly. 'One day, I promise.'

He swirled round, picked up the bracelet from his bedside table and quickly tied a knot in it. 'Give this to your mother. Tell her –' he paused. 'Just tell her, no matter what happens, I never stopped loving her and I never will. Ever. You hear me?'

I nodded, my throat too clogged up to speak. He hugged me one last time before swirling round again. 'Hang on.' He pulled the poem off his wall and handed it to me. 'Give her this as well. Tell her – tell her to keep it till we're together again. Tell her never to forsake me.'

'She won't, Dad. Neither of us will. Ever.'

'I'll find you,' he said again, his voice croaky. 'Now go.' He pushed me through the door. 'Quickly. And be careful.'

I edged down into the corridor and held his eyes for a second. 'See you, Dad,' I whispered. Then he closed the door and was gone.

I wavered for a moment in the empty corridor. The bell was still shrieking – even louder outside the cell. I covered my ears, flicked my tail and got moving. Back along the corridors, into the cleaning cupboard, through the tiny hole, out across the murky darkness, until I found the tunnel again.

Shona was waiting at the end of it, just like she'd said she would be. We fell into each other's arms and laughed as we hugged each other. 'I was so worried,' she said. 'You were gone ages.'

'I found him,' I said, simply.

'Swishy!' she breathed.

'Tell you all about it on the way. Come on.' I was desperate to see Mum. I couldn't wait to see her face when I gave her Dad's presents.

'So tell me again,' Mum twirled her new bracelet round and round on her wrist, watching the colours blur and merge, then refocus and change again, while Millie looked on jealously. 'What did he say, exactly?'

'Mum, I've told you three times already.'

'Just once more, darling. Then that's it.'

I sighed. 'He says he's always loved you and he always will. And he had stacks of poems that he'd written.'

She clutched her poem more tightly. 'About me?'

I thought of the one in my pocket. 'Well, yeah. Mostly.'

Mum smiled in a way I'd never seen before. I laughed. She was acting just like the women in those horrible, gooey romantic films that she loves.

'Mum, we have to see him again,' I said.

'He's never stopped loving me and he never will,' she replied dreamily. Millie raised her eyebrows.

A second later, a huge splash took the smile off her face. We ran outside.

'Trying to get one over me?' Mr Beeston! In the water! How did he get past us? 'After everything I've done for you,' he called, swimming rapidly away from us as he spoke.

'What are you going to do?' I shouted.

'I warned you,' he shouted, paddling backwards. 'I won't let you get away with it.' Then in a quiet voice, his words almost washed away by the waves, he added, 'I'm sorry it had to end like this, Mary P. I'll always remember the good times.'

And then he turned and swam towards the Great Mermer Reef. Mum and I looked at each other. Good times?

Millie cleared her throat. 'It's all my fault,' she said quietly.

Mum turned to Millie. 'What?'

'I loosened the ropes.' Millie pulled her shawl around her. 'Only a tiny bit. He said they were hurting.'

Mum sighed and shook her head. 'All right, don't worry, Millie,' she said. 'Nothing we can do now, is there?'

As we watched Mr Beeston swim off into the distance, Shona appeared in the water below us. 'What's up?' she called. 'Thought I heard something going on.'

'It's Mr Beeston,' I said. 'He's gone!'

'Escaped?'

'He went over there.' I pointed towards the prison. 'I think he's up to something.'

'Should we go after him?'

'You're not going back there!' Mum said. 'Not now. It's too dangerous.'

'What, then?' I asked. 'How will we get back? We've no fuel, the sail's broken. Shona can't tow us all the way back to the harbour.'

'Radio the coastguard?' Mum said.

'Mum, the radio's been broken for *years*. You always said you'd get it fixed at some point – '

'. . . But I kept forgetting,' Mum finished my sentence with a sigh.

'We could always meditate on it,' Millie offered. 'See if the answer comes to us.'

Mum and I both glared silently at her. Ten seconds later, the decision was taken out of our hands. A loud voice wobbled up from below the surface of the sea. 'You are surrounded,' it gurgled. 'You must give yourselves up. Do not try to resist.'

'Who are you?' I shouted. 'I'm not afraid of –'

'Emily!' Mum gripped my arm.

The voice spoke again. 'You are outnumbered. Do not underestimate the power of Neptune.'

Before I could think about what to say next, four mermen in prison guard uniforms appeared on the surface of the water. Each one had an upside-down octopus on his back. In perfect formation, they leapt from the water, their tails spinning like whirlpools. They flipped on their sides, the octopus legs swirling above their backs like rotary blades, and headed towards us. Between them, they plucked Millie, Mum and me from the deck, spun themselves round and held us under their arms as they plopped back into the water.

'I can't swim,' Mum yelped.

For an answer, she was dragged silently under the water. Gulping and gasping, we were shoved roughly into a weird tube-thing. My legs starting turning into a tail straight away – but, for once, I hardly noticed.

We slid along the tube, landing on a bouncy floor. The entrance we'd slipped through instantly closed, leaving us staring at the inside of a white, rubbery bubble. Two masks hung from the ceiling. They looked like the things they show you when you go on a plane.

I grabbed hold of them and helped Mum and Millie put them on. Then we sat in silence as we bumped along through the water. Millie pulled some worry beads out of her pocket and twirled them furiously round her fingers.

Mum clutched my fingers, holding them so tight it hurt.

'We'll be fine,' I said, putting my arm round her. Then in an uncertain whisper, I added, 'I'm sure we will.'

Chapter Fifteen

*T*he good news – they didn't keep us in that tiny, wobbly cage forever. The bad news – they separated us and threw us each into an even tinier one. This time, it was more like a box. Five small tail spans from side to side and a bed of seaweed along one edge. It was all Mr Beeston's fault. How could he have done this to us?

I sat on my bed and counted the limpets on the rocky wall. Then I counted the weeds hanging down from the ceiling. I looked around for something else to count. Just my miserable thoughts. There were plenty of them.

A guard swam in with a bowl of something that looked nothing like food but which I suspected was my dinner.

'What are you going to do with –'

He shoved the bowl into my hands and disappeared without answering.

'It's not fair!' I shouted at the door. 'I haven't done anything!'

I examined the contents of the bowl. It looked like snail sick. Green, slimy trails of rubbery goo spread on top of something flaky and yellow that looked suspiciously like sawdust. Gross. I pushed the bowl away and started counting the seconds. How many of them would I spend in here?

The next thing I knew, I was lying on my side on my horrible bed. Someone was shaking me and I slipped about on the seaweed.

'Mum?' I jumped up. It wasn't Mum. A guard lifted me up by my elbows. 'Where are you taking me?' I asked as he clipped a handcuff onto my wrist and fastened the other one onto his own.

But of course he didn't answer. Just pulled me out of the cell and slammed the door behind us.

'Strong, silent type, are you?' I quipped nervously as we swam down long, tunnel-like corridors and round curvy corners and down more long corridors. We soon arrived at a mouth-like entrance with shark teeth across it like the prison door.

The guard knocked twice against one of the teeth and the jaw opened wider. He pushed me forward.

Once inside, another guard swam towards us. I was attached to a different-but-similar wrist and whisked along a different-but-similar set of corridors.

And then I was thrown into a different-but-similar cell.

Brilliant.

I'd only got as far as counting the limpets when they came back for me this time. And this journey took us somewhere different-but-different. *Very* different.

We reached the end of another long corridor. When the guard pushed me through the door, there were no more tunnels. I was looking out at the open sea again. For a moment, I thought he was setting me free. Except I was still attached to his wrist.

The sea grew lighter and warmer. Something was coming into view. Colour – and light. Not dancing and jumping about like the Great Mermer Reef, but shimmering and sparkling from the depths of the sea. As we drew closer, the lights emerged into a shape. Like a big house. A huge house! Two marble pillars so tall they seemed to reach from the seabed to the surface stood on either side of an arched gateway, a golden seahorse on a plinth in front of each pillar. Jewels and crystals glinted all the way across the arch.

'In there.' The guard gestured towards the closed doorway, nodding at two mermen stationed on either side. They both had a gold stripe down one side of their tails. As the mermen moved apart, the gates slowly opened.

We swam towards the arch. Long trails of shells dangled from silver threads above us, clinking with the movement of the water.

'What is this place?' I asked as we swam inside. We were in some sort of lobby; the sort they have in really posh hotels. Only even posher. And kind of dome-shaped.

Chandeliers made from glassy crystals hung from the ceiling, splashing mini rainbows around the walls. In the centre of the room, a tiny volcano shot out clouds of bright green light – an underwater fountain. The light flowed over the top of the rocky cauldron, bubbling and frothing and turning blue as it melted onto the floor.

'Don't you know anything?' the guard grunted. 'This is Neptune's palace.' He pushed me forward.

Neptune's palace! What were we doing *here?* I thought about all the things Shona had told me about him. What was he going to do to me? Would he turn me to stone?

We swam across the lobby. Two mermen with long black tails passed us, talking hurriedly as they swam. A mermaid looked up from behind a gold pillar as we came to the back of the lobby. Reaching into his tail, the guard pulled out a card. The mermaid nodded briskly and moved aside. There was a hole in the wall behind her.

'Up there.' The guard swam into the hole, pulling me along. Round and round, spiralling upwards through tubes, we climbed the upside down helter-skelter till we came to a trap door. The guard opened it with one push and nudged me through.

We came out into a rectangular room with glass walls. A giant fish tank – except the fish were on the outside! All brightly coloured yellows and blues, darting about, looking in as the guard led me to a line of rocks along one edge and told me to sit down. A notice in front of my row had a word written in capital letters: 'ACCUSED'.

Accused? Me? What had I *done?*

In front of me, there were rows of coral seats. Mer-people were dotted about, dressed in suits.

One wore a jacket made of gold reeds with a trident on his chest. I watched him flick through files, talking all the time to a mermaid by his side. A merman on the row behind them in a black suit was whispering frantically to a mermaid next to him as he, too, shuffled through files.

What was going on? *Why was I here?*

At the front, a mermaid facing the court sat at a coral desk examining her nails. Behind her was a low crystal table – and behind that, the most amazing throne: all in gold, the back of the seat tapered upwards into three prongs filled with pearls and coral, downwards into a solid gold block. The round seat was marble, with blue ripples carved outwards from the centre to the edges. A golden seahorse on either side of the throne: each arm a seahorse body, each leg its tail, stretching downwards and curling into a mass of diamonds at its base.

The throne towered over the court – powerful and scary, even when it was empty!

Every now and then, the mermaid in front of the throne rearranged the items on her desk. She had a row of reeds in a line across the top edge, with some plastic papers beside them. On top of these, a sign saying 'Clerk'. A huge pile of files was balanced in one corner. In the other, a grumpy-looking squid sat with its tentacles folded into a complicated knot.

She kept glancing backwards at a gateway behind the throne. Gold and arched and covered with jewels, like the palace entrance. The gates within it were closed.

A splashing noise opposite me drew my eyes away from the front of the court. Two guards were opening a door in the ceiling; they had someone in between them.

Mum! The guards unhooked a mask from the ceiling, like the ones she and Millie had when we were captured. Mum clumsily strapped it over her face, a tube leading from her mouth up through the top of the box.

She looked round the court with frightened eyes. Then she noticed me and her face brightened a tiny bit. She tried to smile through her mask and I tried to smile back.

What were we doing here?

Outside the fish tank, a row of assorted merpeople were taking their seats. A portly mermaid undid a velvety eel from round her neck as she sat down. She made the others all move up so she could have a seat for an enormous jewel-encrusted crab.

Another huddle of merpeople with notebooks and tape machines chatted to each other as they sat down. Reporters. Along the back of the court, a line of sea-horses stood in a silent row. They looked like soldiers.

Then a hush fell on the room as a sound of thunder rumbled towards us.

As the noise grew louder, the water started swishing about. The clerk grabbed her table, people reached out to grip the ledges in front of them. *What was happening?* I glanced round as I held onto the coral shelf. No one else looked worried.

The waves grew heavier, the thunder louder, until the gates at the front of the court suddenly opened. A fleet of dolphins washed into the room – a gold chariot behind them, filled with jewels and crystals. The chariot carried a merman into the room. At least seven feet tall, he had a white beard that stretched down to his chest and a tail that looked as if it was studded with diamonds. It shot silver rays across the room as the merman climbed out of the chariot. Sweeping his long tail under him, he slid into the throne. In his hand, a gold trident.

Neptune! Right in front of me! In real life!

A sharp rap of the trident on the floor and the dolphins swiftly left the courtroom, whisking Neptune's chariot away. Another rap and the gates closed behind them. A third, the water instantly stopped moving. I fell back on my seat, thrown by the sudden calm.

'U-U-P!' a voice bellowed from the front.

Neptune was pointing his trident at me! I leapt back up, praying silently that I hadn't just doubled whatever sentence I was about to get.

He leaned forward to talk to the clerk, gesturing towards me. The clerk looked up at me too, then picked up one of her reeds. Poking the squid with the reed, she wrote something down in black ink. The squid shuffled grumpily on the edge of the desk and refolded its tentacles.

Eventually, Neptune turned back to the court-room. He stared angrily around. Then, with another rap of his trident, he shouted, 'DOWN!'

Everyone took their seats again as the seahorses at the back split into two rows and swam to the front of the court. They formed a line on either side of Neptune.

The merman in the gold jacket stood up. He bowed low.

'APPROACH!' Neptune bellowed.

The merman swam towards him. Then he ducked down and kissed the base of Neptune's tail. 'If it please Your Majesty, I would like to outline the pros-ecuting case,' he began, straightening himself up. Neptune nodded sharply. 'On with it!'

'Your Majesty, you see before you a mermaid and a . . . *human*.' He screwed up his face as he said the word, as though it made him feel sick. Pulling at his collar, he continued. 'The pair of them have colluded and connived, they have planned and plotted –'

'How DARE you waste my time!' Neptune shouted. He lifted his trident. 'FACTS!'

'Directly, Your Majesty, directly.' The merman shuffled through a few more files and cleared his throat. 'The child before you today has forced an entry into our prison, damaged a section of the Great Mermer Reef in the process – and assaulted one of your own advisors.'

'AND? Is there more?' Neptune's face had turned red.

'It's all in here, Your Majesty.' The merman handed a file to Neptune, who snatched it and handed it to the clerk without looking at it.

The merman cleared his throat again. 'As for the *human,*' he forced the word out, 'the same charges apply.'

Neptune nodded curtly. 'Once again, Mr Slipreed, will that be ALL?'

'Absolutely, Your Majesty.' The merman bowed again as he spoke. 'If I could allude to one outstanding area of this case . . . ' Neptune clenched his fist around his trident. The merman spoke quickly. 'In apprehending the accused, a merchild, acting with the help of another *human* –' he cleared his throat and swallowed loudly – 'was discovered in the vicinity.'

Millie and Shona! I slapped my hand over my mouth to stop me gasping out loud.

'Both merchild and the other are being held awaiting instructions from the court.'

'From the COURT, Slipreed? ANY old court is that?'

'Your Majesty, they await your divine ruling.'

'THANK you Mr Slipreed!' Neptune boomed.

'If I may now call upon my first witness . . . Mr Charles Finright Beeston.'

As Mr Beeston entered the court, I folded my arms. I tried to cross my legs, but remembered they were a tail so I couldn't. He looked different, somehow. As he swam towards Neptune, I realised what it was. I'd never seen him as a merman before!

Mr Beeston bowed low and kissed Neptune's tail. He avoided looking at me or Mum. 'If I may refer to my notes . . . ' A line of bubbles escaped from his mouth and floated up through the water as he spoke.

To your lies, you mean, I said to myself.

'Your Majesty, I was last night tricked into a rescue operation involving a yacht and a small motor boat. I was beaten around the head with a mast and tied up while the accused' – he looked quickly at Mum, then at me. Suddenly breaking his flow for a moment, he looked away again and coughed quietly before continuing. 'Before they carried out their unlawful plans. Thankfully, the accused were amateurs and not equipped to deal with a high ranking professional such as myself.' He paused and turned towards Neptune.

'BEESTON – do not presume to look to me for compliments! CONTINUE!'

Mr Beeston's face reddened. 'Of course, Your Majesty. And so, I disembarked and sought the strong fin of the law.'

'You swam for the guards?'

'Indeed I did, Your Majesty.'

'Thank you.' Neptune banged his trident on the floor. 'DEFENCE!' he bellowed. 'Mr Thinscale? Your first witness?'

The merman in the black suit jumped up. 'Thank you, Your Majesty.'

I looked round the court, wondering who his first witness was going to be. 'Get up,' the guard next to me grunted. 'You're on.' Then he pulled me out of my seat and pointed towards the throne. I swam nervously towards Neptune. Taking my cue from the others, I bent to kiss his diamond-studded tail.

Neptune pulled on his beard and leaned down. 'You understand the charges?' he asked, in a slightly quieter voice.

'I think so.'

'Speak, then!' he snapped. 'Do you HAVE anything to say in your defence?'

'Well, I –' I stopped and looked round the courtroom, and at the merpeople watching on all sides. Some were staring at me. Others were talking quietly or laughing. At me, probably. My tail turned to jelly and I was about to say, 'No,' when I caught Mum's eyes. She removed her mask for a second and forced herself to smile.

'Do not make me wait,' Neptune growled.

That was when I realised what I had to do.

'Um sir, Mr –'

'Do I LOOK like a "Sir"? A "Mr"? Do I?'

I flicked my tail a little, propelling me higher than my one metre fifty, and looked nervously round at the courtroom. 'Your Majesty,' I corrected myself. 'I know this might sound weird, but, well, it's actually kind of nice to be here.'

A murmur flickered through the room and along the rows outside it. The reporters scribbled furiously on their pads.

'"Nice," did she say?' I heard someone ask.

'Is she being sarcastic?' another one replied.

'It's what I've always wanted,' I added quickly. 'Not being in court about to get locked up for the rest of my life, obviously. But being here. With all of you. It feels right.'

I glanced at Mum. 'I mean, I know I'm part human, and my mum's brilliant. She raised me all on her own and everything. But my dad's brilliant, too. Not just because he's a merman, so I get to be part mermaid.' I paused and looked Neptune in the eyes. 'That's absolutely wicked,' I said.

Neptune leaned forward. He scowled, narrowing his eyes at me.

'I mean, it's fantastic – it's swishy! But more than anything, I'm proud of him because of his belief in love.' I pulled the poem he'd written out of my pocket and held it out. 'My dad might have been locked away but his feelings weren't.'

I glanced at Neptune. A tic was beating in his cheek, a glare shone in his eyes, but his body had softened a little; the grasp on his trident had loosened. 'You can't make people stop loving each other just because a law says it's wrong,' I said.

The posh mermaid with the pet crab wiped her eel across her cheek. Another took a hanky out of her coat pocket. A few merpeople were nodding. I heard someone at the back say, 'She's got a point, you know.'

Neptune let out a thunderous sigh and a huge mock yawn.

'My dad fell in love. So what? What did *I* do to deserve to grow up without a father?'

Tutting noises were spreading through the spectators' seats. A couple of them shook their heads.

'I wanted to see my dad, that's all. Is that so wrong?' I paused and looked at Mum. 'If it really is so terrible, if love is such a horrible crime, then fine, lock me up. Lock my mum up, too.' I turned back to Neptune. 'Your Majesty. That merman' – I pointed to the first one who'd spoken – 'he wants us imprisoned because of laws that were written centuries ago. Things have changed. Humans aren't all bad, you know.'

As I looked round the courtroom, I paused on Mr Beeston's face. Neptune remained silent. 'Hey, even one of your top advisers had one for a father,' I said. Mr Beeston lowered his eyes as people turned to look at him. 'If it can produce such loyal, devoted merfolk as Mr Beeston, can it really be so wrong?'

I let my question hang in the air for a moment, before turning back to Neptune. I couldn't think of anything else to say. 'I only wanted to see my dad,' I said finally.

Neptune held my eyes for a few seconds. Then he banged his trident on the floor. 'I will NOT be told my laws are wrong! How DARE you presume!'

He got up from his throne, banging his trident again. Everyone instantly rose to their tails.

The gates behind him opened. His chariot was waiting outside. 'Court will adjourn,' he barked as the dolphins swam into the courtroom. Then he leapt into his chariot and swept out of the court.

I slumped back on my rock and waited to hear my fate.

Chapter Sixteen

*n*o one spoke for the first few minutes. Then, gradually, everyone started whispering quietly to each other, like at the doctor's when you have to act like it's a crime to talk. Maybe it was, here. Everything else was, it seemed.

I returned to my seat and looked up nervously to see if I could catch Mum's eye. She was sitting with her head in her hands. Was she cross with me?

We sat like that for ages, the court almost silent while we waited. Some people left; a few took out lunchboxes and munched on seaweed sandwiches.

Then the gates at the front of the court opened. Neptune was coming back in. Everyone leapt up.

Neptune waved us down impatiently with his trident.

He waited for the court to be absolutely silent before he spoke.

'Emily Windsnap.' He looked at me and indicated sharply for me to get up. I flicked my tail and stood as straight as possible. He looked at Mum and pointed upwards again. 'Mary Penelope Windsnap,' he read from the card in front of him and Mum stood up. 'You have both defied ME, and MY laws!'

I swallowed hard.

'My kingdom has held by these laws very well for many generations. *I* invent them; *you* abide by them. That's how it works!'

I tried to get used to the idea of living in a cell with a bed of seaweed and limpets on the wall.

'Do you DARE say I am wrong? ' he continued, his voice rising with every word. 'Do you think you know better than ME? You do NOT!'

He leaned forwards to stare at me. What would I get? Ten years? Twenty? Life?

He paused for ages. When he spoke again, a gentleness had fought its way into his voice. He spoke so quietly I had to hold my breath to hear him.

'However. . . ' he said, then stopped. He stroked his beard. 'However,' he repeated, 'you have touched on something today. Something beyond laws.' His voice softened even more. 'And therefore, beyond punishment.'

I held my breath as he paused, tapping the side of his trident.

'You will both be released!' he boomed eventually.

A gasp went through the court, followed by a stream of murmuring. Neptune lifted his trident and glared round the room. The chattering stopped instantly.

'You defied my laws,' he went on. 'But why? Shall I pretend I do not understand? Or that I have never felt that way? NO! I am no hypocrite! And I shall NOT punish you for love. I shall NOT! Mrs Windsnap.' He turned to Mum. A long deep sigh, his breath rumbling out from his throat. Then – 'Your husband is also to be released.'

Another gasp whizzed through the court.

'On one condition,' he continued. 'The three of you will join a community on an island with a secret location. This will be your home from now on. If you break this condition, you will be punished most severely. Do you understand?'

He stared at us both. I nodded vigorously. Had I heard right? Was I *really* going to see my dad again?

The gold-jacketed merman suddenly rose from his seat. 'Your Majesty, forgive me,' he said, bowing low. 'But the other merchild? You know, there could be trouble if –'

'Just get them all out from under my tail,' Neptune barked. 'She can join them, for all I care. Discuss it with her parents. Either that or a memory wipe.'

'Very well, Your Majesty.' He sat down again.

Neptune scanned the court. 'And perhaps you can all tell your kinfolk that your king is not only a firm ruler, but also a just and compassionate one.' His eyes landed on me. 'One who will no longer punish folk merely for loving.'

Then he got up from his throne, banged his trident on the floor. 'Case closed,' he bellowed and left the court.

It all happened so quickly after that. The room erupted in noise. People were clapping and cheering; others gossiped among themselves. A few came over to the dock to shake my hand.

'Can I go now?' I asked the guard. He nodded curtly and pointed to the exit as he undid my handcuffs.

Outside the court, a mermaid with her hair in a bun took my hand. 'Your mum will be escorted separately; she'll meet you in a bit,' she said. 'Let's have you out of here.'

'Who are –' I began but she'd turned round and was pulling me towards a boat that looked like a cross between a limousine and a submarine. White and long, with gold handles on the doors.

A crowd was waiting by the boat. 'Emily, can you tell me how you feel?' one of them asked, a black reed poised above her notebook. I recognised her as one of the reporters from the court.

'Emily doesn't want to talk at the moment,' the mermaid said. 'She has to –'

'I feel great,' I said. 'I just can't wait to see my mum and dad together.'

'Thanks Emily.' The reporter scribbled furiously as I was bundled into the boat. There was someone else inside.

'Shona!'

'Emily!'

We hugged each other tight.

'We're going to an island!' I said. 'My dad's coming!'

'Seatbelts,' the mermaid instructed from the driver's seat. Then we shot forwards like a bullet. As we sped through the water, I told Shona everything that had happened. 'And they said you might be able to come, too!' I finished off. I didn't mention the other option. Surely her parents would agree?

'Swishy!' Shona laughed.

'Going up,' the mermaid called from the front as we tipped upwards, gradually climbing until we came to a standstill. Then she opened a door in the ceiling. 'Your stop,' she said to me, holding out her hand. I shook it, feeling rather stupid. 'Good luck, Emily,' she said. 'You're a brave girl.'

'See you soon,' Shona giggled and we hugged each other before I climbed out. I stood on the top of the boat.

Blinking in the daylight, I tried to adjust to the scene. *King* was moored just in front of me. A group of mermen waited in the water in front of it, holding on to two thick ropes. Mum was leaning right over the side, reaching down to someone in the sea. She was holding his hands.

I stood on tiptoe so I could see who it was. For a moment, I thought I must be imagining it. It couldn't have happened this quickly, surely! A mop of black hair, sticking up where it was wet, a pair of deep brown eyes. Then he noticed me and the dimple below his left eye deepened as he let go of Mum's hands and swam towards me.

'Dad!' Without thinking, I jumped into the sea – and into his arms.

'My little gem,' he whispered as he hugged me tight. Then he took my hand and we swam back to the side of the boat together. Mum reached down with both arms and we held each other's hands: a circle; a family.

A second later, a series of splashes and shouting exploded behind us. A bunch of reporters were heading our way.

'Mr Windsnap.' One of them shoved a microphone shaped like a huge mushroom in my dad's face. 'Simon Watermark, Radio Merwave. You've melted Neptune's heart. How does it feel to have made history?'

'Made history?' Dad laughed. 'At the moment, my only feelings about history are that I want to go back twelve years and catch up with my wife and daughter.'

The reporter turned to Mum. 'Mrs Windsnap, is it true that your babysitter helped with your plan?'

That was when I noticed Millie sitting on a plastic chair at the front of the boat. One of the mermen was perched on the deck opposite her, his tail dangling over the side, the pair of them frowning at a pack of tarot cards spread out between them.

'We couldn't have done it without her,' Mum said.

The reporter turned to me. 'Emily. You're a brave girl to do what you did. You must have had some help along the way. Is there anyone you'd like to say a special thank you to?'

'Well, I'd like to thank my mum for being so understanding. I'd like to thank my dad for waiting for us.' He kissed my cheek. 'And Millie for falling asleep at the right time.'

The reporter laughed.

'And I'd like to thank Shona. My best friend. I could never have done this without her.'

Out of the corner of my eye, I saw a familiar figure. Merpeople were talking and laughing in groups all around us, but he was on his own. He looked up and smiled a shaky, crooked smile at me, his head tilted in what looked like an apology.

And I forgave him.

Almost.

There was just one thing he could do for me first.

He jumped a little as I swam over to him. I whispered my favour in his ear.

'A mass memory wipe?' he blurted out. 'That's ridiculous – not to mention dangerous.'

'Please, Mr Beeston,' I begged. 'Think about all

the nice things I said in there. After everything that's happened, I should hate you forever. But I won't. Not if you do this one little thing for me.'

He looked at me hard. What did he see? A girl he'd known all her life? Someone he perhaps cared about, just a tiny little bit?

'Very well,' he said eventually. 'I'll do it.'

I kept my head down as we stood by the side of the pool. Everyone around me chatted in groups. Julie was with Mandy, giggling together in the corner. Fine. I didn't need Julie. I had Shona and no one could be a better best friend than her.

My heart thumped in my ears, blocking out everything else.

Bob arrived. I stepped forward, put my hand up. 'Please, sir – I'd like to show you something.'

Bob frowned.

'I've been practising.'

He waved a hand out. 'All right then,' he said with half a smile. 'Let's have it.'

I stepped towards the edge of the pool.

'Look at *fish girl*,' Mandy sneered from the corner. 'Showing off again.'

'That's right,' I said, looking her right in the eyes. 'Fish girl is showing off.'

198

I glanced up to the window. Too high. I couldn't see out, but I knew he'd be out there. He promised.

I had five minutes. Five minutes to be proud instead of scared. Five minutes to be free, to be myself. But mostly, I had five minutes to give Mandy Rushton the biggest shock of her life!

And so I dived in. Piercing the surface as gently as I could, I swam underwater all the way to the opposite end of the pool.

'Big deal!' Mandy snorted. 'So fish girl can do a length underwater. Whoopedee do!'

As she mocked me, something was happening under the water. My tail was starting to form. The familiar feeling filled me with confidence. This was it!

I dived straight down. And then, I flicked my tail up in the air. Spinning round and round under the water, I could feel my tail swirling and dancing, faster and faster. I couldn't wait to see Mandy's face!

I swam up to the surface, wiped my hair off my face and looked across. Thirty open mouths. Total silence. If they'd been playing musical statues, it would have been a dead heat.

Mandy was the first to step forward. 'But – but –' she sputtered. 'But that's a – how did you –'

I laughed. 'Hey, guess what, Mandy? I'm not scared of you – and I don't care what you call me. You can't stop me being who I am. And you don't get to bully me any more, because I'm leaving. I'm off to a desert island, with a whole bunch of – '

A loud rap on the door stopped me saying any more.

Bob walked over to it in a daze. Mr Beeston. Right on time. He spoke quietly to Bob. 'Of course,' Bob said, his voice flat and mechanical. 'I'd forgotten. Come on in.'

He turned to the class. 'Right, folks, we have a visitor today. He's come to give us a special talk.'

Mr Beeston stood in front of the class, a large bag in his hand. 'Now then, children,' he said. 'Listen carefully. I'm going to teach you about lighthouses – and the dangers of the sea.'

He opened the bag. 'But before we start, let's all have an iced bun . . .'

I slipped quietly out of the pool as Mr Beeston held everyone's attention. It was almost as if I'd been forgotten. I would be soon!

'Thank you,' I mouthed as I passed behind the class. He nodded solemnly in reply.

I crept away from the pool, changed quickly and slipped outside. Looking back at the building, I smiled.

'Bye 7C,' I whispered. Then I turned and walked away.

We left that night. Mum, Dad and me, off to a whole new world where who knew what was waiting for us. All I knew for sure was that my life as a mermaid had only just begun.

But remember, it's just between you and me.

Lots of people have helped this book make its way from my computer into your hands. I would especially like to thank:

Mum, for getting rid of all the pounding hearts and lurching stomachs;

Dad, for noticing all sorts of things that everyone else missed;

Peter B, for the title;

Kath, for her eagle-eyed nitpickiness;

Helen, for everything I've learned and gained from working with her at Cornerstones;

Cameron, for lending me books about sea life with great pictures and fantastic facts;

Cath, who hasn't actually had anything to do with the book, but has been a brilliant pal all the time I've been writing it.

With extra special thanks to:

Lee, for an inspirational friendship, and for being so in tune with me and my characters;

Jill, for sharing the journey, and for having endless discussions about mermaids without complaining once;

Catherine, for all her support and guidance, and for finding Emily such a good home;

And Judith and Fiona, for being the perfect editors.